Enterprise." He ends ~~~
and warning, obviousl~~~
myself. I finally bring ~~~
and I have to stop my ~~~
up in a sharp well-tail~~~

ning man I have ever laid my eyes on. His brown hair is shaved short on the sides and slightly longer on the top— long enough to run your fingers through— and I wince slightly at how his green eyes watch me with burning intensity. Why the fuck is he looking at me like that. Just as I'm about to gear up with my flashy *'I'm the President daughter's smile,'* his lip curls up in disgust.

Fuck being polite to this prick. The way his cocky eyes narrow on me, he obviously knows how hot he is, which means, I won't be fueling that ego.

He's maxed out of ego fuel.

I look to my father and watch as his eye twitches in slight annoyance.

Great. Fuck my anal cavity.

"Hi." I lean over the table, placing my hand out to him with a very forced and very toothy smile on my face. I mean, you could count all my teeth from across the room, that's how wide this smile was. "I'm Isa."

He looks to my hand, then looks up to my face, then back to my hand. Said hand is getting very tired waiting for his prick hand to accept. His angular jaw clenches a few times before his penetrating eyes pierce through mine with such hate, I almost flinch. Don't you fucking flinch.

Flinch.

Fuck.

"Bryant." His voice. I wish it was ugly and ratty. However a rat would mutter the word 'Bryant,' but I wish it was like that. Instead, it was like, you know when you take

that first spoonful of a molten lava cake, and the moist—
yes, I said moist—cake melts away on the tip of your
tongue, right before your taste buds get the ride of their life
with the rich creamy sauce that begins to slither down your
throat?

Yeah. His voice was like that.

I tug my hand away, slightly ashamed at how obvious he
was at rejecting me. What the ever-loving fuck did I ever do
to him. Or maybe someone pissed in his million-dollar
cornflakes this morning.

Clearing my throat, I bring my glass up to my mouth,
eradicating any thoughts about his sexy voice. I can't believe
I compared his voice to a molten lava cake.

What an insult to the cake community.

I sip my wine, just as my father starts talking with Bryant
about some trade deal in the PNW (Pacific North West)
when my phone vibrates in my purse. I smile sweetly at my
dad, even though his attention doesn't stray from Bryant,
and unfold the flap to my purse, pulling out my phone.
Swiping it unlocked, I open up to a text message.

How are the Hiltons?

I smirk at my best friend's text message before shooting one
back.

What are they ever? **Perfect and all that boring shit.**

Lydia clears her throat rather obviously and bumps me

Crowned by Hate

Crowned Duet: Book One

By Amo Jones

Cover: Jay Aheer from Simply Defined Art

Editing: Ellie McLove"

CROWNED DUET: BOOK ONE

CROWNED

BY

HATE

USA Today & Wall Street Journal Bestselling Author

AMO JONES

"To all the fuckers who said I would never amount to anything.
grins
Sup."

I sa, pick your chin up and smile. I taught you better than that."

"I'm twenty years old, Lydia, not fifteen. I know what I'm doing."

Swooping up my wine glass, I empty the contents down my throat.

"Well, I beg to differ. Why can't you just be like your sister?" Lydia quips, eying me up and down.

"*Well,* I don't know, Lydia," I mutter sarcastically while smiling politely at a passerby. Because it's one of the nights my father gives me and my sister the pep-talk to behave ourselves, I have to be on my best behavior. Only he doesn't need to drill everything into Brianna's head like he does mine, because she understands it. She knows how to handle herself—apparently I don't, being the delinquent and all. But, I don't see her here tonight. Oh no, perfect big sister is shacked up studying Harvard Law.

See.

Golden child.

"Maybe it's because I have a thing called a backbone and a mouth?"

"That's a cheap stab at your sister and you know it, Isa. Stop this." My eyes go over Lydia's ridiculously perfected chiffon bun and land on my father, who has his salt and pepper hair slicked back to show his strong features and bright blue eyes. My dad was strapping when he was younger, but age has not been kind to him. Or maybe that's karma.

"My favorite girls." He grins, his arms stretched out wide.

"Great," I murmur from around the rim of my glass. "Dad is extra cheesy tonight."

A foot hits me under the table and when I look up to Lydia, I catch her glaring at me. See, keeping up appearances is what my family is all about. Since my father not only has his fingers in all sorts of dealings in the US, and by dealings, I mean he's a shady individual, he's also the president of the United States of America—*blah blah*, that's why it's imminent that I'm on my best behavior constantly, and even more so while we're at one of the many events we attend together as a 'family.' Family is a strong word to use, though. What I have, is more like a business gathering where we all barely tolerate each other—not so much a family.

My father continues to walk toward us, pulling out a chair beside his and then taking a seat. Another figure catches the corner of my eye, but I don't look toward it because I'm too busy counting the new wrinkles that have carved into my father's forehead, though it probably looks like I'm openly glaring at my dad in annoyance. I can neither confirm nor deny this assumption.

"Isa, I want you to meet Bryant Royal. The CEO of Royal

under the table with her leg—again. I look to her and she widens her eyes at me. She's a little unbearable at times.

I'M at a rage right now and have the biggest cock you could imagine rubbing up against my leg. Oh, Isa, oh, Isa, you have to feel his mon—

I CHOKE ON MY DRINK, my hand flying up to my mouth to stop it from escaping. *Jesus, Devon!* Lydia pats my back in a *nice* gesture—well, *nice* to people who don't know that she's a bit savage on the best of days—and says in a soft tone, "Are you okay, dear? You almost got your drink everywhere!"

I smile apologetically at her, and then offer that same smile to my father, and then furthermore to Bryant, though his includes a slight clench of the teeth. "Yes, so sorry about that."

Bryant leans back in his chair, propping one elbow onto the armrest and runs his index finger over his upper lip. "Something funny, huh?"

My dad shuffles in his seat, watching me carefully and Lydia's eyes snap to mine. I can see them both glaring at me carefully out the corner of my eye. They're both probably praying I don't say something sassy that will land my ass in hot Royal water.

"I suppose so," is all I answer, pulling away from his annoying fucking gaze. I hate the way he has been watching me. It makes me a little uncomfortable, and I don't know why. He reminds me of someone or something. Something calculating. Something I've only witnessed on someone once in my life.

Red alert. We aren't going there right now.

I glance back to him once I realize he hasn't replied back to me, only to find him flicking an unlit cigarette around in his mouth. Yeah, I'm pretty sure you can't smoke in here. He reaches into his pocket, flicks open his Zippo, and lights up his cigarette. Taking a long inhale, his eyes flick to mine, a smirk tickling the corner of his lips. Thick grey smoke slowly leaks out between his cocky lips.

Now it's my turn to ask questions.

"Something funny?" I tilt my head my head and cock my eyebrow.

His grin deepens before he shakes his head, blowing the remainder of the smoke out through his mouth. "Nothing that concerns you."

"Ho—"

"—So, Bryant, how was the game last weekend? Was a tight run in?" My dad interjects, knowing what I'm like and how I struggle to keep my mouth shut. Not to mention, you could pretty much cut the tension between Bryant and I with a pair of scissors—it's that thick.

Rolling my eyes, I snatch my purse off the table. "Excuse me."

Pushing past all the expensive frocks, fake tans, hair extensions, and dollar-dollar-bill bitches, I finally walk through the doors and step outside, letting out a long breath. God, why do I feel like I just survived The Hunger Games—foreplay version. Probably because I just did. That man had me hungrier than Katniss Everdeen right before she almost got ganked for stealing those bags of food.

My phone vibrates in my purse and I quickly grab it out.

"Hello?"

"You didn't answer me, I thought you might have been dead."

"Nope," I pop the "p," taking my smokes out of my bag

and putting one in my mouth. "Sorry, still here." I light up my cancer stick and take a long inhale before blowing out.

"You need to quit the cigs."

"You need to quit sucking dick every day but hey! What do I know." My best friend is bi. He tends to swing both ways. I love him to bits for many reasons, but one of them is definitely because of this. He has never cared what people thought nor has he cared for labels. If he finds you attractive —and I don't mean that in a shallow way, I mean that if he finds you attractive in any way, he will try to sleep with you, and he usually gets his way because not only does he look like he should be on the cover of GQ magazine, but he has the gift of the gab too. He could sweet talk a nun into removing her panties in record time.

"What time are you bringing your sexy ass home?"

"I'm leaving now."

Hanging up my phone, I put it back into my clutch before pressing my fingers into my mouth and whistling for the first taxi I see speeding toward me.

A sharp ringing sound pierces through the dark depths of my dreams, so I groan, flipping over onto my tummy while squeezing the pillow to my ears. "Make it stop!" The nuisance doesn't stop though, oh no, it continues.

"Isa!" Devon—the best friend—storms into my room, the door handle hitting the back of my bedroom wall.

He snatches my phone from my bedside drawer and flashes it in front of me. "Answer your fucking phone."

He must see that I'm not about to answer my phone or him, so he answers, "Hello?" Devon groans down my phone. "Yes, ma'am." The mattress dips from underneath me. "Isa!" he whispers harshly. "It's Lydia, wake up!"

"Sorry, I'm dead," I murmur, snuggling deeper into my warm blankets.

"You asked for it..." something drops to my bed and then he walks out.

"Isa! Are you still asleep? It's midday! For goodness sake, woman, get up!"

I let out a throaty groan while shoving the blankets off myself.

Fucking Devon, putting my phone on speaker.

Massaging my temples, I close my eyes. "Yes? What do you want!"

"The charity auction is tomorrow. I expect you to be here. Both your father and I do..."

"I can't. I have work." I flip my warm squishy blankets off my body.

"You're an artist. Your job is not that important. Reschedule."

I swing my legs off the bed and pull my ruffled socks up my legs. "My paintings don't allow me to reschedule. Sorry, the creative brain curse, it means we're a slave to ourselves." I walk into my closet and tug down a pair of tight ripped skinny jeans and a clingy off the shoulder crop top. I have a slender body with a bubble butt and double DD's. Devon says I have the body all men crave and all women envy, I'm not sold. I have wide ass hips and tiny legs. That means, when I buy a size two in jeans, they're almost always tight around my butt while being loose around my waist. But these jeans are my favorite. They're washed denim with a couple holes in the knees of each leg. They're my favorite because they tuck and shove all of my skin in, and by skin I mean fat. The crop top is for added innocence since these are practically hoochie jeans.

Taking out a pair of nude strappy heels, I dump everything onto my bed. I wonder if this top will go with those dashing hoops I bought last week. Why am I caring what goes with what ou—

"Are you listening to me, Isa? You need to attend. Your father has important men coming tomorrow, and we need the family together!"

"For what— exactly?" I shuffle out of my loose cotton shirt, throwing it across the room. I'm not a tidy human. It drives Devon crazy, but I think it's good for him to realize if he ever decides to settle down, that not all woman—or men — are uptight little OCD clean freaks. Some of us, don't care.

Some of us, think there are more important things to waste your time on. Like I don't know...eating.

"For the election, Isa, for goodness sake. You know your father is in his second term running for the presidency. You need to support this family whether you agree with some of your father's decisions or not, it's imperative that you attend. Especially with the end drawing near."

"Jeeez." I clip my strapless bra on. "How much did he pay you for that speech?"

"Isa..." she exhales. As much as I love to ruffle my step-mom's feathers, deep down, I don't want to overly-stress her out. My father does that enough for both of us.

"I'll be there, Lydia." Picking up my phone, I hang up and toss it back onto my bed just as Devon waltzes back in with his gym shorts hanging casually off his hips and a tight tank clinging to his chest.

Around a mouthful of granola, he points with his spoon. "You're looking much more awake."

My eyes narrow. I know it's not his fault, but being mad at Devon is always fun, and anyway, now I'm in a pissy mood in general because I have to fucking fly to Washington.

"You got sucked in, huh?" He grins at me around his spoon, his boyish dimples sinking into his cheeks. Devon is handsome, that's a given. He has thick lashes which curve around his ocean blue eyes, a messy mop of blond hair, and a hint of a smooth golden tan that I'm guessing, he inherited from his part Spanish background.

"Only because I didn't want to be a pain to Lydia." A guy walks past behind Devon down our hallway, and I snap my eyes back to a guilty looking Devon.

"And who was that?" I add a quirked eyebrow.

"That?" he looks over his shoulder innocently. "What?"

"Devon!" I bite at him.

"It's not as—" another person walks past him, only this time, it was a girl.

"Really?" I deadpan. "You *had* to go there?"

He grins at me, his baby blue eyes lighting up my room and enough to break through my pissy mood.

I sigh in defeat. "I'm just jealous. I haven't gotten any in well... almost a week." Collecting up the rest of my clothes, my head slightly hanging between my shoulders. In this day and age, the word 'Nymphomania' is tossed around about as much as said 'nymphos,' but I truly believe both Devon and I suffer with this condition. Both for different reasons. I don't know much about Devon's family life. In fact, any time I ever asked about his family he always shut down, but I know my reasons have a lot to do with my home life. You know, 'she wasn't loved enough as a child' *blah blah*. It's all fun and games until someone *really* wasn't 'loved enough as a child.' I have issues. Deep issues that I run away from by the temporary void sex gives me. I'm working on it, I guess. But if I'm being honest, I haven't gotten much better.

"Well..." Devon places his bowl on my dresser, coming further into my room. I watch as each muscle clenches with every movement. "You know I can scratch that itch, baby."

"Don't!" I hold a single finger up. "I'm not... no. I'll be okay. I'll go out with Jen tonight."

I could go out with Jen, but in all honesty, a night out with Jen isn't always a good time.

"Baby, you *know* you need it..." Devon begins, inching

toward me. "You need to find you a daddy. One who will not just rock your world, but fucking smash it into pieces." Devon starts air humping the post of my bed, and I toss my shirt at him. "Get out!"

I need a new best friend.

Once he finally leaves, I tug on my jeans, jumping up and down to squeeze the goods in and then throw my shirt over my head. Walking into the bathroom, I fluff my dark hair up until it falls in natural waves down to my tailbone. I quickly dust on some make-up, I don't wear much of it and hardly wear it so it's all cracked and old. Brushing on my mascara, I chance a real look at myself in the mirror. I wouldn't say I was unfortunate in the looks department, but I have insecurity issues that I fight with every day, which is why, in short, I have sex with men because it makes me feel good. It fills a void that was left inside of me when my mom abandoned me and my nonexistent father decided that his career was more important than raising his daughter. So yes, I enjoy sex. It's something that makes me feel good—what's so wrong with enjoying that? I'm so sick of the slut-shaming in this day and age. A girl gets called a slut if she has the sexual appetite of a man. Well, I'd wear that badge with pride and polish it with my middle finger.

Exhaling, I place my mascara back into my make-up bag and look back at myself in the mirror. My eyes are a deep green, almost like greenstone, while my skin is more on the paler side — thanks to my mom's Scandinavian heritage. I do have my father's angular jawline and his small pixie nose. I think. I've only ever seen one photo of my mom and it was an old image of her and my dad sitting around a dinner table. The photo was in color—I'm not that old—but it's the only time I've ever seen a photo of her. I have her skin and eyes, from what I could see. Maybe even her black heart.

Shoving my phone into my back pocket, I head out of my bedroom and into our tiny living room. We live in a small apartment in the French Quarters of New Orleans, but my parent's house—outside of the Whitehouse, the house I grew up in— is in Greenwich in Connecticut. So every time I have to fly home, that's a two-hour flight. Lydia always pushes me to use my father's private jet, but I'd be much more comfortable traveling amongst civilians just in case someone decides to shoot my father's plane down or something crazy like that. Running for second term presidency, we have Peter S. Johnson. Aka, my dad. Though he's never been overly active in my life as a teen, he's still my dad. He stands for family values but doesn't seem to have any himself. Figures. In order for him to keep up appearances and keep his unscathed name peachy and squeaky clean, I have obligations. It's unfortunate really, and it's why I moved to New Orleans in hopes to leave all this behind me, or rather, run away from it all. But no matter how fast and how good I am at running—

"One of your MIB taking you to the airport?" MIB is code for Men in Black. Sometimes, Devon will even drop down and sing his own version of the Will Smith song.

Yep. Secret services. The president's daughter gets zero play time. It's why, occasionally, (maybe like three times), I have done a solid runner. Before I can answer Devon, my phone beeps and I slide it open.

Isa, Jerry will take you straight to the airport. Try to be early, please. You're a headache for all the workers.

Ahhh, now by workers, I'm guessing she's talking about my friend Daniel who is also the pilot of our private jet. This is my father's second league running, so all the workers are well acquainted with me. I send a message back to Lydia.

(rolls eyes)

Not funny, Isa.

(double rolls eyes)

....

See you soon.

I giggle, tossing my phone back onto my bed. She has a point, and I shouldn't be making the workers' life extra hard. Truth is, most of them have been around me more than my father because he's just never home. After gathering up the last of my things and tossing them into my suitcase, I yell out, "Devon!" while scooping my hair into a high ponytail.

He saunters into my room with a towel wrapped around his torso. Water is still cascading down his rippling muscles, and I swear to God, fucking steam I still floating off his skin. The sweet smell of his soap hits me instantly, and I come hither him. "My family stressed me out." I end with a pout.

Devon grins, gripping the edge of the towel and dropping it, giving me a full display of his athletic body. His thick cock falls into the palm of his hand, all angry and hot.

He pumps himself once, pulling his bottom lip into his mouth. "Come wrap your lips around me, Isa, and suck me good like I know you can."

I walk toward him, dropping to my knees while looking up at him from under my lashes. "Always." Then I wrap my lips around Devon's length, sucking on him slowly and licking around the rim of his cock. Peeking up at him, I slowly suck him deep down my throat. He groans, gripping my hair and tugging my hair back until the tip of his cock is resting on my plump lower lip. He grips his dick, rubbing his tip all over my lips.

"God, I want you to be mine, Isa."

Ice fucking water. Nope. No. I inch back, my mouth slamming shut and my jaw tensing. "You know the rules, Devon. Say something like that again and I'll find someone else to fuck me."

He growls softly. "Fine. Get on the bed."

I obey, and Devon does what he does best. Making me feel good, wanted, sexy. All until I can't feel my legs and I almost miss my flight. Oops.

3

Slipping on some Jimmy Choos, I straighten my tits in my dress and run my nude lipstick over my lips one last time. As soon as I landed yesterday, I crashed at a hotel. Jerry and his MIB's probably would have rather I be at the White House, you know, thus making their life and job a little easier, but the less time I spend with my dad, the better. For my own sanity.

"Thanks, Jerry!" I knock on the glass separator in the back of the limo, fluffing up my hair. It cranks down, and Jerry's eyes come to mine in the rearview mirror. "I'll be a few minutes. Behave yourself, Isa."

"Aw," I tease, giving him a small wink. "I always behave myself, and anyway, what could I possibly get myself into at the palace?"

He sighs, and then the separator is closing. I guess that conversation is over. I shouldn't give Jerry such a hard time, but I'm guessing he's used to it now what with almost five years dealing with me. Sighing, I gaze out the window as we pull in. I hate this place. It represents all things that I'm not. I'm not superior, nor do I think I am. I know that not all presidential candidates are like that, but my father, though he has America's best interest at heart – always—is. He seems to leave his kids—my sister and I— to fend for ourselves almost all of the time. Or, he likes to think that all the men he has employed will do it for him. Which they do – every time. More Jerry than anyone else, but I always have at least three secret service agents following me around twenty-four seven. I've played poker with Jerry. He has chased away my one-night stand guys who wouldn't leave my apartment. He has answered my cell phone when other guys never got a clue that I wasn't interested, pretending to be my Navy Seal husband. In that regard, though, Jerry would be way scarier than any Navy Seal. My sister, on the other hand, isn't as much hard work. She has her own MIB's that follow her around, including her very own Jerry, who goes by the name of Chan. I'm truly not sure whether his actual name is Chan, I've just always called him that because he resembles Jackie Chan, and I never cared to know what his real name was. She's the poster child for my father. Harvard law student, articulate, smart, classy. Everything that I'm not. I don't think I'm *not* smart, but I believe more in doing something that sets your soul on fire than something that will make you miserable just to keep your father happy. That's not me and not what I'm about at all. I tried, when I was younger, to satisfy my father and be something that he could be proud of, but every time my sister was around I would get tossed under the mat, so eventually, I stopped trying. I slowly started to realize that I don't need to rely on family to make me feel wanted. There are lots of different ways you can make yourself feel good. Never rely on anyone else for that.

One of the security personnel pushes open the front

door for me, so I walk in, slamming it closed just as the strap
of my shoe comes undone.

"Shit, shit, shit." Running my fingers through my hair to
push the mass of brown strands out of my face, I hop up and
down like a maniac while trying to fix my shoe. Eventually,
my bouncing around moves me toward the back of the
house where there's a huge tent set up for the event. I'm still
not sure what event this is for—charity, I think Lydia said.

I'm still attempting to push my damn shoe on when I see
how many people are here. Finally, I hook the little buckle
back into its hole, swiping a glass of wine from a passing
waiter before downing it in one go. These things are bad for
my diet, not because of all the food, but because of all the
alcohol I consume.

"Isa." One lady nods her head in passing. She's wearing
a bright red dress that screams *'I'm important'*, but I don't
know who the fuck she is, so I smile. "Hello," I respond
with my own head nod. I'm so terrible at this. Maybe I was
adopted or swapped at birth. I've always felt out of my
element at these things despite the fact that I've been
around it all my life. I have never been able to get used
to it.

I look toward the front of the marquee, taking another
sip of my wine when I stop. My skin blazes to life, the air
gets sucked out of my lungs and the soft melody of whatever
bullshit song that was playing disappears into the background of my heavy breathing. There, standing next to my
father deep in discussion, is Bryant Royal. *The* Bryant Royal.
When I say *the*, I mean *the* egotistical ass from the other
night. Can I say he was an ass, though? I mean he didn't
really out rightly be an asshole to me, but his whole "I'm
Lord" attitude pissed me off, so yes, I'm sticking to he's an
arse. My father looks as though he's talking his ears off,

though. He sure is fond of Royal. I can't help the snarky chuckle that leaves me.

Just as Bryant brings the rim of his glass to his lips, his eyes swoop to mine and then he pauses with his glass halting just short of his mouth. A sexy stupid grin tugs on the edge of his lips as he slowly tips his glass to me in a small gesture before downing all its contents. Why is it the more I see him, the more I think he looks familiar? I can't even trust my own brain, though, because there are times when I meet people and I think I've seen them before, but it turns out, they just look uncannily similar to someone I've seen on television.

It's probably just because he's 'Bryant Royal.'

I do a small curtsy to him *Jesus fucking Christ. Why the fuck did I just curtsy him?* Maybe because he's fucking American royalty. Yes, I've done my research. As soon as I got home after that dinner, I Googled "Bryant Royal" and was surprised what came up.

Bryant Saint Royal
  Twenty-seven years old.
  Youngest New York mogul to hit US soil in decades.
  Russian roots.
  CEO of Royal Enterprise Holdings.
  "Bryant Royal is American Royalty and is our very own high flying bachelor. Never pictured with the woman once, we wonder how such a man keeps his activities so private."

YEAH OKAY, so I googled a little deeper than what would be deemed appropriate. Bryant's cold hard eyes go back to my father, obviously ignoring my witty curtsy and continues his conversation. Swallowing the rest of my spritzy champagne, I head toward the table laid with food. Second best thing about these things—the Champs being number one—is the food. I'm picking at a bunch of grapes when my dad calls out to me from across the room.

"Isa!" My father's voice feels as though it ripples through the room.

I stop my greedy food grabbing and turn to face him slowly. "Yes?"

"Come here for a second." He come-hithers his index finger. I widen my eyes slightly at my father, and then slowly glance around the room, remembering where I am. Remembering I have to behave myself. I don't need to cause a scene here, and I don't want to. I try to pick and choose my fights with daddy-dearest, and this isn't one of them.

"Crap," I mutter annoyingly under my breath, just as another waiter passes me. I quickly swoop up another flute, bringing it to my mouth as I make my way toward them.

"Hmmm?" I murmur around the rim of my glass, just as I reach their table. My eyebrows raise slightly in defiance, but admittedly, that's more aimed at Bryant than my father.

"This is Bryant Royal."

Jesus, now he's getting Alzheimer's.

"I know, Dad. I met him at the charity thing a couple nights ago." I take another long—very, very long— gulp of my wine.

My dad brushes off my response. "He's the reason why we're throwing this party, Isa, pay attention." Wait. Pay attention? Is he joking, I haven't missed anything at all.

"Sorry." I am not sorry. Bringing my hands to my mouth, I swipe at the small drop of champagne that fell onto my lip, and I'm just about to end my sentence with something sarcastic, when I again, remember where I am. I really,

really, hate these fucking things. Tilting my head, I humor them both. "And why is he throwing *this* party *here*?"

"Because he's just made a large settlement, and it's *here* because I offered." My father looks to my wine glass. "How many have you had?" 'Large settlement' I have learned, is code for 'this-is-something-important-that-little-people-won't-understand,' and I'm cool with this, because I really, really don't care.

"Not enough." There's a slight snap in my undertone when I reply before I finally let my eyes rest on Bryant. "Congratulations on your...*settlement*." Whatever the fuck that means. "Excuse me," I murmur, side-stepping away from Bryant and moving to the other side of the tent to raid the buffet. I can't pass up free food. Piling small finger food onto my napkin, it's not long before someone clears their throat from behind me.

I crank my head over my shoulder slightly, a grin tickling my lips when I see who it is. "Yes? Can I help you?"

Bryant steps closer to me, his hands going into his pockets. He narrows his eyes. "Yeah, actually, you could."

"Oh?" I pop a grape into my mouth. "Do go on, your *highness*."

His eye twitches, but he keeps glaring at me, and it feels like hot fire searing through the glacial glades of the Antarctic. I'm not sure how that would feel, but I'm guessing it would be this. His razor-sharp angular jaw clenches before his dark eyes find mine quickly. "You're going to do me a favor."

I chuckle, turning my back to him and snatching another bunch of grapes. "Why on earth would I do you a favor?"

I feel him before I see him. His hard chest slightly presses against my back, enough to light up everything that is in the direction of south, but then his breath falls on the nape of my neck and his strong hands grip around the curve of where my waist sinks in, and I find my thighs clenching together. "Because I have something you want." He shoves me into his groin. Not enough to alert passersby, just enough force to tell me he's not playing around.

My eyes slowly close and my head tilts to the side softly, stupidly asking for his touch. "And what might that be?" It comes out as a small whisper. Damn it. Would I sleep with him? Hell. I'm pretty sure I've woken up to worse.

"They should call me wolf..." My eyes snap open and a light panic begins to pulse deep under my flesh. There's no way. I would remember him—I would surely remember. Though, I don't remember much of those days.

Tensing, I spin around to face him again, my eyes burning with so much intensity I hope he shrivels in his very spot. "What the fuck are you talking about?" Fuck. Please. Please let this be some bullshit game. He's bluffing, he's gotta be.

Bryant cracks his neck, a devious grin pulling across his mouth. He smiles politely at a passerby, before bringing his attention back to me. "Summer 2012. That night ring a bell to you?"

My chest contracts. Fucking contracts like a woman's uterus right before she's about to birth a fucking ten pounder. I look down to the floor, trying to do the math, but the swirly patterns that are encrypted into the soft plush rug all begin to blur and the room...holy mother of shit, the room begins to spin slightly.

Gripping onto the corner of the table to stop me from falling, I whisper out, "Wh-at? This—this doesn't make any sense."

Shrugging, he swallows the rest of his wine in one

smooth movement, his Adam's apple bobbing softly and his lips glistening from the wine that had slid over them. Placing his empty glass back on the table, he brings his bleak eyes back to mine. "Yeah, that was me. Amongst the others, if you remember anything at all, that is... So here's the deal..."

I flinch back my tears. I am strong. I am wild. I am a survivor.

I think.

Fuck. Are you still a survivor if you can't remember the darkest part of your memories? Or does that make you a coward by nature, that even when you don't realize it, your body is spinelessly burying shit that it knows you couldn't handle. But even so, all the hard work I put into forgetting that night, forgetting what I'd done and how bad I had gotten, it all meant shit now because all it took was for him to say one little word, one word—*Wolf*—and all feelings, all the hurt and pain I felt was beginning to all come back tenfold. I bring my cold eyes up to his, a new-found hate, a hate so strong it overpowers my legs wanting to wrap themselves around him. "What?" I snap, grinding my teeth together. "What do you want."

Bryant's dark eyes search mine eagerly, a sadistic smirk skimming across his lips. "You marry me, and I'll make sure no one ever sees the tape."

"What!" I cough loudly before a spastic of fits erupt from my throat. "Excuse me, but *what*?" I drop to a deathly whisper, inching myself closer to him. "And what fucking tape are you talking about?"

"You don't ask questions," he adds, smiling at another person walking pass as if he didn't just tell me I was going to fucking marry him and that he possibly has evidence to some very disturbing shit that happened years ago.

"See, that won't work for me. I'm a question asker," I retort, my lip curled in disgust.

"It will have to work."

"Huh." I shake my head. "If you have anything of that night—"

"—Stop thinking, and I do have shit from that night. You know within yourself that I do. Look into my eyes, Isa." he comes closer to me, but my hands fly up instinctively, pushing him away.

He ignores my push as if It's nothing, and cocks his head. "Who am I?" He looks between each of my eyes, a cocky smirk tilting the corner of his mouth. "Who," he whispers, leaning forward until his warm lips brush over my earlobe. "*Am I*," he ends harshly into my ear, his warm breath ticking over my flesh.

I close my eyes. *Fight it, Isa.* "Fuck you, don't tell me what to do."

There. I showed him.

"Great start, baby, come..." he places his hand out to me.

"Nope." I shake my head. "I need proof that what you're saying is true, and also! My dad, my best friends, they're not going to believe I fell in love with your pretty fucking eyes the first time I saw you. They know I'm smarter than that." This is true, though I can't see my father arguing it, in fact, if I didn't know any better, I'd say he orchestrated the whole thing—that's how much he adores Bryant.

Bryant shrugs. "Then just tell them it was my cock. Bet they'd believe that."

My face scrunches in offense, but then my frown falls. "Actually, they're probably more inclined to believe that." Sad, but true. "But I will still need proof. That video, what happened that night, your friends," my voice drops to a low whisper, "no one can know. *Ever*." There's one part of that night I remember vividly, and that's the part that I'm guessing Bryant has evidence on.

His eyes search mine. "Oh, I'm well aware how much you wouldn't want people to know what happened that night. Tell me..." he steps forward until his lips are skimming over my jaw, "do his dead eyes haunt your dreams at night?" My breathing stops, and my lip trembles. Stepping backward, I search his eyes. "I know who you are," I whisper, searching his eyes. It's him. It's Wolf. Even though he looks different now, I will always remember those eyes.

He grins again, his eyelids heavy and his eyes dark. "Say it."

I open my mouth, but then close it, not wanting to entertain his bullshit games. "Let's go. I need to see this fucking tape." Snatching my clutch off the table, I leave my wine. My poor, innocent wine. Just as I'm about to step forward, his hand catches mine, tugging me backward forcefully. "Nah uh, baby." He steps closer, his arm wrapping around my neck to pull me under his arm. "We need people to start questioning our actions for this to be believable. It starts now." He kisses the side of my head as we start making our way back toward my father. My skin is crawling from the remnants of memories he's left floating around me. My whole attitude has changed. I no longer care about the wine or the food, I just want to see the fucking tape.

I plaster on a fake smile anyway, forcing myself to melt into his hard body. Over the years, I've mastered the art of the fake smile. "Dad," I announce as soon as we come near. My father looks between both of us with confusion, but I see the moment when understanding sets in. My dad knows me. Knows I've never hidden the fact that I have a healthy sexual appetite so he would think that I've just seduced Bryant into some of my shenanigans. That is, of course, if he hadn't orchestrated this, which if I go by his response to seeing Bryant's arm around me, is a solid no.

"Yes?" He can't even try to hide his joy. Cheers, Dad, just another thing to add to your 'Best Dad Ever' list.

"We're going to leave, is that okay?" I continue with that Oscar-worthy smile.

His face lights up, obviously pleased with what he thinks, is going to be my next bed partner.

"Of course. I'll see you both tomorrow."

Bryant smiles, his hand falling onto my tailbone where he presses down softly. "Thank you for throwing such a successful night, Peter."

My dad smiles appreciatively and nods in excitement. Idiot. My father is an idiot. Well done, America. "Of course, Bryant. It's a great cause to contribute my time to."

We both say our goodbyes to the few people who Bryant wanted to say goodbye to and then walk back through the main foyer, smiles still on our faces and our bodies still twisted around each other. Passing questioning looks from the workers and a few attendees, we push through the large front doors, and as soon as my feet land on the tiled steps, I pull away from him instantly, letting the cold air of the night trickle over my now hot flesh. "Don't touch me again!"

Bryant chuckles. "Yeah, sure, say it like you mean it next time." He hands the young valet boy his parking ticket and the young boy looks back at Bryant in adoration, smiling. "I won't be long, sir."

Stupid fucking kid.

4

I sa! Come here for a second!"

Brooke yelled from across the field, so I began walking toward her, swallowing what was left of my beer.

"Whatsup?" I slurred, tossing my empty red cup onto the dewy grass.

"So check it." Brooke chuckled, coming closer to me, close enough for her drunken breath to skim over my cheek. "Those guys there," she tossed her thumb over her shoulder to indicate where a group of about five guys were standing. All different sizes and heights. I couldn't see that much because my vision was blurring in and out. I looked back to Brooke, her bright blue eyes glaring into mine with a gleam. "They know where we can really party."

"'Really' party?" I asked, eyebrow quirked. "And what exactly did they say?" Brooke leaned in closer, her lips coming over the lobe of my ear. "Where we can fuck for as long as we need." I stepped backward, then looked over her shoulder to the guys again, this time focusing my eyes more. Well, attempting to. They were now all similar heights, but different builds. One caught my eye briefly, but I didn't lock onto him for too long.

"And if we get murdered?" I asked Brooke, a cheeky smile on my lips.

"Then we die happy."

Shrugging my shoulders, I smirked. "Life was for living."

PULLING UP TO A HOTEL COMPLEX, Bryant veers the car into an underground parking area. The silence between us is deafening, and if I wasn't so fucking confused and mad, it would have made me a little uncomfortable. He switches the car off just as I turn in my seat to face him. "I don't remember much about that night. I mean, the smaller details I'm not very good at. Some PTSD shit, but..." I trail off, narrowing my eyes onto his. "Wolf."

Bryant grins, running his hand over his short stubble. "Yeah. I'm sure we can work on getting the rest of your memories back. Come on." He pushes open the door, getting out and leaving me in the empty car alone. I stall briefly, a wave of panic and distrust washing over me before I decide that I have nothing to lose, and maybe some lost memories to gain, so I push the door open. "Well, lead the way."

He stops and then stares right through me. Just when I think he's going to say something, he shakes his head and chuckles before walking toward the elevators. "Well okay," I mutter under my breath, following him. The doors ding open and I step in, watching Bryant closely.

"So why?" I ask, folding my arms across my chest.

"Why, *what*?" he pushes the 'PH' button and the elevator starts rising.

"Why didn't you ever turn me in?" He looks at me on the corner of his eyes, his jaw clenching.

Wanting to look away from his penetratingly annoying

gaze, I cock my head forward, just as the elevator doors ding open displaying the vast space of immaculate dark marble tiles, red shaggy rugs, and floor to ceiling windows that overlook the bright city lights. The lighting is soft, falling over us in a dark orange shadow. I step forward. "Wow." Looking toward the kitchen, I turn around to face him again with a small smile playing on my lips.

"Nic—" my lovely view of his apartment is rudely cut short as something is shoved down over my face. A scream erupts out of me from my panic just as I feel a rough hand squeeze over my mouth as another wraps around my head, tugging me backward. Swinging my legs around, I try to kick, scratch, and claw whoever it is that is behind me but with no success.

"Fuck!" The voice growls. "B, knock her out. She's too feisty!" A thud vibrates against my head just as a dark abyss pulls me into a deep slumber.

"Are you sure this is a good idea?" I asked Brooke, just as we walked back toward the group of guys. "I mean, I'm drunk, high, and horny, and I'm all for a good time, but..."

Brooke halted, turning to face me as her hands came to my shoulders. "Trust me, it's fine. They're hot, a few years older than us, but imagine, just imagine, how good they are in bed!" Brooke's eyes sparkled with excitement as she sucked her bottom lip into her mouth.

I ran my tongue over my suddenly dry lips. "Fuck it. Let's do it." Brooke and I had been friends since we were fourteen. We both had issues, man issues, we were both addicted to sex. To the feeling and attention, that we got during sex, so it was only a matter of time before we became friends. Even at such a young age, we knew. She has been there for me through some of the loneliest days of my life.

Once we reached the guys, I smiled suggestively toward them, but I'm not sure what it would have looked like because of all the drugs and alcohol that was zipping through my body. I felt like a ten, but I probably looked more like a solid two.

Swiping open the doors of the tent, I shoved Brooke aside with a grin. "You ready for this?" I still haven't thought really hard about how they managed to have this all set up here. It must have taken a load of men to set it all up.

She shrugged, taking off her shirt and shifting the bottle of Jack from one hand to another. "Born ready, bitch." I peeked inside the tent and saw the guy I noticed earlier with a smirk on his face. He was handsome, but it was more in an obvious boy-next-door way.

Heading to where he was lounging on an armchair, I wrapped my arm around the back of his neck and lowered myself down onto his lap. Bringing the rim of the bottle up to my lips, I tipped the bottle back and swallowed. "Hey."

He grinned, two dimples sinking into each cheek. "Hey."

Looking from his eyes to his mouth, I brought my lips down to his, skimming them over and running my tongue across the rim. "You wanna play with me?"

He tucked his shoulder-length blonde hair behind his ear. "Yeah, I'll play with you."

"I'm a little broken..." I added, smirking darkly.

"Broken girls fuck better."

I laughed, gripping the back of his neck and yanking his lips to mine. Pulling his bottom one into my mouth, I sucked on it roughly all while sliding off his lap. "Yeah, we do."

MY HEAD THUDS like a pounding pulse is strumming heavily

through every vein inside of it. With blackness clouding my vision like thick fog, the rich scent of tobacco, sweet cologne and leather dominates my senses. Bringing my hand up to my head, I yank the black rag off, tossing it onto the ground. Rubbing the blur from my eyes, my vision catches the rich mahogany wood, deep blood red walls and sleek black side desk that's hidden in the corner. Walking toward the single bed that's pushed against the wall, I run my hands over the silk sheets until the material is slipping over the palms of my hands. I'm so stupid. Of course he wanted me dead. I killed his—whatever he was to him—they'd all want me dead. I was so caught up in being in the safety of having my father's name over my head that I completely lost touch with reality. Of the fact that dangerous, sick guys who liked to do sick things in bed, might want my head. Do I regret that night? Yes and no, but do I regret that night for the reasons I should? No. Why does Bryant want to marry me though? Why? Why go through all this if he's just going to kill me in the end?

The light from the hallway shining through the opening of the door breaks through my expanding thoughts. Bryant walks in, shoving his hands into the pockets of his slacks.

"What the fuck do you want from me?" I whisper, though it comes out hoarse.

Pulling out a packet of Camels, he bangs the end onto the palm of his hand until a single cigarette pops out. Bringing the packet to his mouth, his eyes stay on mine as he bites down on it, tugging it free with his teeth. He flicks open a metallic black Zippo, inhaling deeply before letting the thick cloud of smoke slowly leak from between his lips.

I wave it away, trying not to inhale what feeds my addiction for nicotine. Oh, how I could do with a smoke right now. "What I want, is for you to do exactly as you're told."

"I can't do that. Never been the submissive type."

He chuckles, though it's not a nice chuckle. It's a chuckle that has chills erupting over my spine. Looking to the side while taking another long inhale of his cigarette, he growls, "These are non-negotiable terms, Isa, and from what I remember, you do the submissive thing very well. It just takes a particular type of man to bring your stubborn ass to your knees."

"Why?" I blurt out because it's the first thing that pops up in my head. "Why? Why would you need me? Why wouldn't you just turn me into the police, or hell... kill me?"

His sharp jaw clenches as he flicks the ash off from the tip of his smoke. "The latter is still up for discussion."

I swallow. "Well, just get it over with then."

Bryant laughs, dropping his smoke to the ground and stepping on it with his perfectly polished dress shoes.

"Why would I make this easy for you?" He tilts his head. In an instant, his hand comes up to my neck. He runs the tips of his fingers over the curve of my jaw before hastily gripping onto my throat and shoving me against the wall roughly, my head smashing against it. "You killed my brother."

N o...
that
was—
"

"—My brother..." Bryant repeats, his hand closing around my throat again until I can feel the small bones in my esophagus crunching. "You killed him."

"You were all sick, demented! He killed himself... he... he..." I can't finish my sentence.

"Fucked filthy?" Bryant answers for me, tilting his head with a cocky grin on his face. "So tell me, if he had stuck his dick inside you while whispering sweet nothings into your ear instead, would you still have lodged a knife through his jugular vein? Was it just because he didn't tell you what you wanted to hear? Is it because he fucked you ruthlessly?"

"I said to stop..." I whisper, my throat clogging up from pent-up emotion. "My number one rule was if I said to stop, you stopped..."

"What was *our* number one rule before you stepped into that tent, Isa?" Bryant edges, coming closer toward me.

I flinch, his grip tightening around my throat. "Answer me!"

"Fuck! That I don't step inside the tent unless I agree that I have no limits..."

"No. Fucking. Limits." He releases my throat, pushing me onto the ground. "It wasn't until he actually fucked you that you decided you had a limit. And then when he didn't listen, you killed him." My breathing thickens until I'm reaching for my throat in an attempt to release what feels like fog that has been caught up right at its apex. My chest rises and falls as I look around the room restlessly, trying to find clues. The perfect answer, maybe? I fucked up though. I made the biggest mistake of my life and I've lived with the secret since.

"I didn't..." I shake my head, choking out a hoarse whisper. "Fuck! I didn't mean to!" A single tear slips over my cheek but I swipe it away angrily. "I didn't think that would be his kink! Hell, I didn't even know people had a kink like that!"

"Isa!" Brooke yelled at me and I turned to face her, unlatching from the man's neck.

I widened my eyes as in to gesture what it was that she wanted, but she ignored me, nudging her head over her shoulder toward the opening of the tent. Rolling my eyes, I swung my leg off his lap before dragging my index finger over the side of his face. "I'll be back." Walking toward the door, I muttered, "This better be important," to Brooke just as I pushed the door open and stepped into the cool air. Brooke walked out a few beats later and started pacing back and forth, her palm pressed against her forehead. "I need more drugs." Finding out what she needed and that it wasn't all that important, I shoved her out of my way,

ready to walk back inside again. Her hand came out to stop me.
"Isa..."

Searching her pleading eyes, I decided to squash whatever anger I had toward her and her crack addiction. "Fine!" I huffed. "Come on." I turned back around and started heading toward our car where we had a bag of coke waiting for us. She needed it, whereas I just liked to play with it.

Pulling open the door, I gestured toward the passenger seat where she sat down.

"You don't want any?" she asked, opening the glove compartment and taking out a bible, a razor, and a hundred-dollar bill. Sounded like the start of a great love story.

"No, I'm good. Just hurry up." I looked up to the tent, hoping no one could see us.

After Brooke had hit a few lines, she got out of the car, so I shut the door, turning to find all the guys had followed us, now they were all standing watching us from the door. I began walking toward them.

"Wait!" Brooke grabbed my arm, tugging me backward. "Are you sure you're up for this? I mean... I am, but they seem..." she cast a look over my shoulder, her eyes scanning over each of the guys before coming back to mine. "A little intense."

"Intense is a good thing, remember? Intense means they fuck good!"

Brooke grinned, hooking her arm into mine. "You're right, and I do like a good thrashing!" Her British accent came in strong as we headed back toward the guys.

I stopped in front of the one with the long hair whose lap I was sitting on, ignoring the other two. He pushed his hair out of his face, displaying his milky white skin and bright blue eyes. "There will be rules upon entering..."

I grinned, running my tongue over my bottom lip. "And what are those?"

"Well, not those, really just one," he continued, his eyes raking over my body.

"No limits," a voice behind me growled, a voice I hadn't yet met. The deep vibrations of it had me turn at its command.

He was beautiful. Too beautiful. His body was built for a soldier.

"Oh?" I took my eyes back to the long-haired guy ignoring the beautiful beast. "That's fine. No limits..."

We walked inside the luxurious Moroccan tent and I peeked over my shoulder, grinning at the guys who were watching me from the entrance. "Well, come on then..." I teased, winking at them and stepping inside.

Brooke bounced through their bodies, tying her hair up into a ponytail, her blue eyes twinkling with mischief. I turned back around and finally took in the surroundings a little better this time. The four-poster bed that's sitting in the corner, the red silken sheets blanketing it, just screaming sex club. I headed toward one of the posts and ran the palm of my hand over the varnished wood, my fingertips skimming over the intricate pattern imprinting the wood. Taking in a deep breath, I ignored the sweet tang of rich mahogany and cologne dancing together in a room that was quite obviously built for fucking. Closing my eyes and then opening them, my head tilted and my eyes zoned into a large cage that sat in the opposite corner of the room. Stepping closer, I ran my palms over the cool metal, just as I felt a presence behind me, his breath falling over the nape of my neck. "You wanna play, baby?" I recognized his voice as the guy with the long hair.

Pulling my bottom lip into my mouth, I cranked my head over my shoulder a little while my hand glided down my belly, toward the apex of my thighs. "I'm always ready to play."

Twisting me around, he wrapped his arm around my waist, instantly bringing my body into his until my forehead smacked *against his chin. Laughing slightly, I peeked over his shoulder to see Brooke already on her knees, unbuckling one of the other guy's pants as the new hot mysterious guy from outside sat lazily on a large leather seat with a bottle of whiskey dangling between his fingers. He loosened his tie, his dark brooding eyes locking onto mine briefly. My brain fuzzed, my sight started coming in and out of focus from whatever drugs we had taken earlier. Fucking smart idea that was... again, Brooke's idea of partying is so much different than mine.*

"Make her bleed," the new guy on the sofa growled. I decided to call him Wolf. He suited that name. His mere size, his commanding glare, his everything, was almost wolf-like. Calculating. Deathly. Just him being in the room made the temperature both drop and rise all at once. His lip curling up in disgust as his eyes assaulted my body snaps me back to reality. "Make her bleed and then fuck her."

I swallowed, the challenge both terrifying me and exciting me all at once. Looking back up to long-haired guy's eyes, I tilted my head in question, a slight smile on my lips.

Leaning down, he murmured against my cheek, "Orders are orders, Isa..."

"Wait... how'd you know my name?" The ground looked as though it had started spinning from under my feet. Fucking drugs. Alcohol? Mix of both? What happened...

"Oh... we know everything about you, baby girl." Long hair grinned in triumph, then he cast a look over his shoulder toward Wolf, and then that's when his face changed. His features fell in submission, but he quickly collected himself, clearing his throat. "What? You told us."

Brooke. Bet it was fucking Brooke. He took my hand and tugged on me roughly until I fell into his soft chest. Wasn't my ideal lay, but whatever, I can make it work— His hand instantly came to my throat, gripping it roughly until all air had been robbed.

"Get on the bed." I began stepping backward until the end of the bed collided with the back of my legs. He shoved my chest so hard my back hit the mattress in a heap and my hair sprawled out from underneath me. Crawling up my body, he gripped my blouse and yanked at it until all the buttons flew off.

"No tapping out, baby girl. You're my toy now."

"OH, you knew exactly what you were doing..." Bryant murmurs, stepping forward. "You were that little slut looking for dick..." he pauses, a smirk on his mouth. "But you almost got the whole gang." He pauses, coming up to me again until his chest brushes against mine. "We were kids then, so I can understand your slut chapter. What I want from you, though, it isn't revenge. I do want it eventually, but I'm a businessman first."

"Which means?" I snide at him, my lip curled.

"Which means, I need you as my *wife*."

"Why!" I lean back onto the bed. "Why, aside from who my father is, would you need me to be your wife?" I pause, looking around the room. "You have everything," I whisper, more to myself. "Money, fame, power...what could I possibly give someone who has it all?"

His laugh breaks through the eerie silence. "Revenge in the sweetest way possible. I'll make your life a living hell while gaining the benefits of marrying the president's daughter."

"What benefits?" I knew his plan was to make my life a living hell. Why not. I killed his fucking brother.

Yet again, he steps closer toward me and then leans down to cage me in with his arms. "I need you to bleed for me every fucking night. You game for that?" He cocks his head. "Of course you are because you don't get a fucking choice." His hand comes to the back of my head as he clutches my hair into his fist, yanking my head back until his eyes are looking deep into mine. "Now get the fuck out of this room, take a hard right turn until you get to the stairs, walk up those stairs..." he halts, his lips brushing over mine until I feel his smirk press against my lips. "Strip, and get on your fucking knees."

His voice and glare activates my deep, dark addiction. Looking up at him, I suck my bottom lip into my mouth. "Okay..." I gasp softly, entranced in the spell his eyes have put me under and the feelings, those feelings, the crave to be desired and wanted, it all comes crashing back into me.

"Yes, *what*?" He licks his lips devilishly.

I grit my teeth, my stubborn nature fighting to come through. "Yes, sir."

He unlatches from my throat and points to the door. "Do as you're told."

I make a beeline for the door, pausing for a split second to glance over my shoulder at him. "I'm sorry, Bryant. For what it's worth..."

"It isn't worth much more than your pussy, so get the fuck up there and be waiting for me on your knees."

Asshole.

Super fucking asshole.

I turn back toward the hallway, slamming the door closed behind myself as thoughts hammer through my brain with every step I take. I head up the dark gloomy hallway with memories, regrets, and sadness latching to me.

I don't really regret what happened that night, and I think that makes me a bad person. Well, at least half of a bad person. I just wish that it had turned out differently for him, for all of us. I wish I didn't have blood on my hands – but I do. Now I have to live with it for the rest of my life. Though I thought I had suppressed most of the guilt I had through hours and hours of therapy, it obviously doesn't take much to set them off again.

Walking up the stairs, I take the first right turn like Bryant instructed, coming face-to-face with a sleek black door. Running my fingers over the smooth marbling, I close my eyes and let out a heavy breath. But no matter what I try to do, all the memories have started flooding my brain again. Memories that were buried under all the hurt and regret I had spent years upon years building on—slowly crumble inside of my brain.

HE PULLED out a knife from his back pocket and ran the blunt side up my leg.

"What?" I asked, as his thumb pressed against my clit again. I'm confused at what he's doing, or asking, if he even asked something. Did he ask something?

"Shhhh," long-haired guy murmured while continuing to drag the knife up to my pussy. "Actually, fight it." He grinned, pressing his lips to my ear. "That's how I like it."

I swallowed, my mouth dry and coarse from my sudden come down off the drugs.

"I don't want to anymore." My head shook from side to side, just as the cool metal continued to press against the inside of my thigh, only this time, a sharp sting erupted from my inner leg. I scream so loud I almost deafen myself while flinching away from him. I felt the wetness trickle down my inner thigh but slammed my eyes closed, attempting to cut them out. Cut them all out and this whole night. It's not happening. It's not that bad. You're just having a bad trip, Isa.

"*Too bad it's too late to make that decision,*" he quipped back, standing from the bed and flicking the knife around between his fingers. He peered down at me and cocked his head, his eyes running over my body in a way that had my flesh crawling. I turned from left to right, trying to make sense of what was happening, though nothing really did make sense. Nothing at all. A sharp sting stabbed into my outer leg this time, causing a monstrous scream to erupt out of me. I got to my elbows to see what the fuck it was. That shit was painful. I think I'm going to die. I'm going to be an episode of '*1000 Craziest Ways to Die*' or whatever it's called. People will be sitting in the comfort of their home, watching how a stupid drugged up sex addict got herself into a difficult situation all because orgasms. A needle was sticking out of my bare thigh— "*Is that?*" my vision blurred even more, the colorful Moroccan décor now swimming in a murky pool of colors.

"*Heroin? Don't worry, it's just for trial.*"

"*What did you do?*" I heard a voice growl out in the background.

I knew that voice. I thought I did, at least...

"*Oh come on, B. We're just having a little fun with her.*"

"*I said make her bleed, not drug her.*"

"*Just go with it.*"

There was a long pause, so I laid backward onto my back, the wires in my brain now coming to life. The large drapes that hung on the roof of the tent began to twirl and twist into a trance, and I giggled, my hand coming to my mouth. Nothing about this was funny, yet I found myself floating on a magical carpet of peace. Everything felt as though it was going to be okay. No worries, no stress, no actual thought process running through my brain. Just bliss, momentary peace. The sharp sting on my thigh no longer throbbed in pain, I now felt nothing.

"*There you are.*" Long-haired man stood on the side of the

bed, unlatching his belt. He tugged his jeans down until his cock sprung free. Thick and hard, and usually, the sight would have my thighs clenching together. Usually, I would be feeding off of his lust like a sex maniac sponge being tossed into a bath full of hormones, but it didn't do anything for me sexually. My emotions were heightened from the drug cocktail, but it made do the opposite of what he was probably hoping for.

"No." I shook my head from side to side. A fit of giggles sounded around the room. It sounded like a pack of hyenas were around the bed, waiting to feast on me. I brought my head up to see three faces coming in and out, doubling up in blurry sights, then just as they all laughed again—all but Wolf— their faces began to morph. Their faces slid out long, their heads shaping into one of a hyena, their eyes dousing blood red now and their shoulders rose up to their necks as their laughter got louder. I was tripping. Majorly tripping and I wanted out.

"You," I whispered out harshly, looking straight at Wolf, his eyes glaring into mine. "Your name should be Wolf." I look back to the sudden hyena hybrid humans that circled around my bed, just as long hair guy spread my legs wide and removed my panties. "No," I said again, shaking my head and now bringing my attention straight to him. He came in and out, but black heavy dots threatened to steal my vision.

"Oh, lies, we know it's all lies." He spread my legs wider, coming between them and resting his body weight over mine. Another stab came from the inside of my other thigh and I let out a blood-curdling scream. That was when I felt it. His cock slipping inside of me, invading my walls with every single inch of himself. Of what I didn't want. I said no. Tears poured out of the corners of my eyes. I was getting raped, wasn't I? Or is it my fault for putting myself in this situation? Either way, though I can't gather any coherent thoughts, I could now feel something. Something clear.

Pain.

Survival.

Physically and emotionally. I wriggled, my weak attempt at trying to get him off me but it wasn't useful. He was too large and I was too drugged and obviously, injured.

"That's it, baby, move with me." He pulled out, then pressed back in. Bile rose in my throat and the acid hit my tonsils like a dose of reality. Though I was still drugged, the buzz felt as though it was dying out a little. Maybe it wasn't heroin, or maybe it was shit heroin, or maybe I'll probably die from the shit heroin that he pumped into me, so for that reason alone, I wouldn't go down without a fight, but I wouldn't know what heroin felt like anyway. It's not a drug I use, or will ever use. I was still out of it a lot though, and weak, but my mind felt a little more aware, and just as I realized this, the pain in my thighs intensified like a panic alarm. I wriggled again, leaning toward the side to check my leg, but through the blurry vision of my tears, all I could see was red. Red smudges all over my upper thighs. Oh this was bad.

I looked up to catch Wolf just as he turned and walked out of the tent.

"Get off me. I said stop."

"Nah uh," he grunted, sweat dripping onto my face. "I say when it's enough." He launched his fist into my face, dazing me a tad but not enough to knock me out, just before he ran the knife down my leg again. Terror erupted over every inch of me.

Pure, undiluted terror.

"Please," I begged. "Please stop." His disgusting cock slowed inside of me and I went to move my leg, only it was numb. He raised the knife to his mouth and licked my blood off the blade. "I said—" I raised my hand, and in one fast movement, I gripped where his hand held onto the base of the knife, twisted it and then stabbed it through his throat. I let out an earth-shattering scream as his blood rained down over my face. Blood seeped into my eye

sockets and leaked into my mouth. My retribution was now dancing on the tip of my tongue.

Everything after this went in slow motion. My scream cut out once I realized what I had done. I had killed someone. Oh my God, I killed someone. My chest began to rise and drop as an electrifying pulse of panic zapped through me, jolting me to consciousness. The undeniable pain in my thighs no longer mattered. I killed someone. Took a life, and now that would hover over my head until my days were over. I could never undo what I had done. Realizing that his body was still on top of me, I tried to push him off again but he didn't budge, though it didn't matter because the other guys were already there in a flash. The door flew open and Wolf barged back in, his eyes finding the body slumped over mine. One of the other guys pulled him off me and I shot off the bed, blood strewn through my hair and seeping into my pores as my own wept out of the two wounds on my thighs. Wounds that no doubt would need stitches. But none of that mattered. I had killed someone, taken a life. Collapsing to the floor with sobs wracking through my body, I let out the floodgates. Brooke dropped down beside me and wrapped a blanket around my shoulders. "Everything will be okay, Isa," she whispered into my ear, but it was no use. There was no use.

Wolf stood in front of me, looking down his nose in disgust.

I dropped my head between my shoulders. "Take me in."

When he didn't answer, I slowly looked up at him again, peering through my blurry vision.

"No," he replied, his voice deep. A voice that would otherwise have no emotion, but I heard something then. He was affected, though could I blame him? I had killed his friend. "You can live with this for the rest of your life and just when you think you're living again? I'll be there to remind you, now, get the fuck out." I didn't move, though, not until Brooke started getting to her feet slowly with her hand wrapped under my armpit.

I killed someone.

"Now!" he roared, and my body immediately responded. I shot to my feet, wincing at the pain just as Brooke threw my arm over her shoulder and leaned. "Come on. I know someone who will be able to stitch that up."

6

The door slamming brings me out of my dark thoughts, but it's too late, I'm rocking in the corner, reliving my most horrific memories over and over again like a vivid live movie that won't shut up in my head. Wrapping my arms around my knees protectively, I continue to rock softly in the corner while swiping the tears off of my cheeks. I've swiped so many tears off of me already that it now feels as though my cheeks have been scrubbed with sandpaper. How'd I not peg Bryant before? How'd I not notice those eyes. I mean, his body is visibly larger now, more muscular, more manly, and his hair is styled differently. Back then, he also kept his face clean of any scruff instead of the shadow he now has, but those eyes. They should have been the giveaway. Had I buried those memories so deep into my consciousness that I had forgotten those eyes?

"Do you regret it?" Bryant's dominant growl sets off shivers down my spine, his body hidden in the shadows.

"Regret killing him?" I ask through a shaky voice. "Yes,

because it was a life. I don't regret what I've done, though. He should have stopped."

Bryant walks closer into the room, out of the shadows slightly, and drops something into the bedside dresser. "Is that what you tell yourself when the nightmares get to be too much? Hmm?" He adds, pulling open a draw.

I shake my head. "No," I whisper. "I've not had an episode in some time."

"Then you are a heartless bitch. Which is good, because what we have, you don't need a heart for. Get the fuck up, arch your back, and touch your toes." I instantly get to my feet, ignoring the pang of pain I feel deep in my chest.

"Where do you want me?" I ask softly, bringing my cold eyes to his. It's like stone facing stone as the soft light from the lamp casts shadows over his chiseled jaw, enhancing the intensity of his glare.

"I want you naked, on your fucking knees, and at my feet. Do it." Clenching my jaw and fighting my instant reaction to say something sassy in response, I slowly pop the buttons off of my dress, watching him watch me.

He steps backward, loosening his tie before throwing it across the room into a pile of mess on the floor. He unbuttons his pale white dress shirt until his ripped chest comes into display. When he turns to show his back, every muscle has been worked and then worked again. I haven't seen Bryant naked, but he has large tattoos on his back, one in particular that perks my attention. It's a large tiger that claws up the back of his neck. His muscles flex and bend as he moves his arms, rolling his shoulders like he's gearing for a fight. Dropping my dress to the floor, I shimmy out of my lace panties and kick them to the side until I feel the cool winter air whisk over my nipples. Keeping my eyes on his back, I drop to my knees as instructed, placing my hands behind my back. His bare feet come into view, the bottoms of his slacks hanging around his ankles. Clutching a fist full of my hair, he tugs on it roughly, yanking my head back until I'm looking up at him from the floor.

He searches my eyes. "You don't speak unless spoken to, you don't fuck unless instructed to, and you sure as fuck don't let those pretty little eyes land on any other man. Are we clear?" I don't answer because as much as I know how much of a dominant he is, I fight it. I'm not the submissive type, I'm a little too fiery to just bend over and obey, but I have a lot of myself riding on this...situation. Until I can find whatever it is that Bryant has as proof against me killing his brother, I have to play along in this sick and twisted little game.

"Yes, we're clear."

I swallow and go to stand to my feet, but he stops me by clutching my chin with his hands all while his other tugs on my hair until my head cranks back further. "Now," he murmurs, a smirk coming across his mouth as his tongue slips out and licks across his bottom lip. "Show me what that pretty little mouth can do." Bringing my eyes to the front of his pants, I tug down his zipper, pulling his briefs down until his cock springs free. Wrapping my fingers around his large, warm, length, I slowly suck him into my mouth. Letting my tongue pave and moisten every single bit of his thickness before I slip out, lick my tongue down his shaft and all the way to his balls. Working his cock with my hand, I slowly suck one of his balls into my mouth, massaging it softly with my tongue before popping it out. Running my tongue further, I bring it down to where the skin bridges from his balls to his ass, and then circle his ring slowly. His cheeks tense, his grip tightening.

"What are you doing?" He narrows his eyes down on me, tugging my hair gently but not telling me to stop.

"Let me play..." I answer from between his thighs before slipping my tongue into his ass and circling it.

"Fuck," he growls in surprise but grinds his dick into the palm of my hand. "Keep doing that, baby. Harder."

I do. I shove my tongue in harder, circling it when it's inside before his knees begin to tremble. He pushes me back and my ass hits the floor in a thud. "That was fucking hot, but I'm in charge here." He bends down, grips me from under my shoulders and throws me onto the bed until my small frame bounces up from the impact. Crawling up my body, he pulls out a small switchblade from the bedside drawer. It's small but looks sharp.

He grins, his straight white teeth flashing across his face. "Time to play, baby."

"Well, ok, but last time that didn't end well, so..."

He shakes his head. "This is how *I* play. I'm not into drugging girls to get them into bed." I flinch, but he carries on. "And anyway, as I said, I'm in charge."

He brings the knife up to my inner thigh, running the blunt side across my flesh teasingly, torturing me with what's to come. Small memories dance across my brain because he's treading dangerously close to the scar on my thigh. When suddenly, it's gone. The sensation of the unknown has disappeared, so I open my eyes, only to find him on top of me, his eyes watching me so intensely it's almost unnerving.

Almost.

"Close your eyes," he commands.

I do as I'm told, just in time for him to pull, what feels like a blindfold over my eyes. "Now, spread your arms wide. I'll need you locked down for this." I don't know why, but I do as I'm told, spreading them far until I feel a cold metal clamp around each of my wrists. He tugs on them, bringing them both up toward the headboard where I hear two metal clinks on either side of the posts. The darkness from being blindfolded and the lack of control from being bonded to the bed has kicked up all other senses tenfold. My skin electrifies to life from the mere whisper of breeze what whizzes through the room from a cracked window, and the silence that hangs between us could lick over every inch of my screaming flesh. He presses his cock into me while bringing the tip of his nose down to mine.

"Isa..." he mutters, his breath falling over my cheek. I feel the tip of the blade come up my leg again. "Don't flinch, or I'll use a bigger one."

I listen, unmoving. I don't want a bigger one, I barely want this one. It should make me uncomfortable. If I were normal, this would be classified as a hard limit because of my history, but it's not. It.... Excites me. Maybe that's one of the many reasons why I'm fucked in the head. My deep breathing begins to drown out any other sounds, just at the point the blade drags against my tender thigh. Bryant's breath moves from my face, trickles over my jawline, down my throat, and over my breastbone before he presses his lips against my flesh. "Don't fucking move." I obey, completely submissive in the bedroom against my own will. He continues his travels, drawing his tongue out and licking his way down, past my belly button and against my pelvic bone. One of his hands slides down my leg until he clutches my ankle, spreading my legs wider. The tip presses into my thigh, but away from the scar. There's a sharp sting that stabs into me just as Bryant covers my clit with his mouth, licking his tongue over my clit softly. The sharp stab of the blade somewhat intensifies the pleasure in my apex as the trickle of blood seeps over my thigh. Bryant pulls away, the cold air whipping over my pussy and now my aching leg. I'm thankful in a way that he didn't cut the same place his brother did all those years ago. I haven't been able to touch that area, let alone let another person inflict pain there. His thumb presses against my clit just as his hot mouth opens against the pain in my leg. He suckles over the wound like a vampire would his last feast, biting down on my flesh roughly as his thumb increases pressure, circling me continuously. My back buckles from the bloom of pleasure I feel building in my core, about to shatter under his very touch. Just as I think I can't take anymore, his mouth replaces his thumb and I'm done for. One-hundred thousand bombs all set off at once, shattering heavens doors open until fucking angels sing and it feels like drops of fire rain down on me. My orgasm rips through my body with my legs quivering and stars dancing in front of my blacked out vision. Coming down, his finger dives inside of me and circles around, running it over the skin between my pussy and my ass. He presses the same finger to my lips, dipping it into my mouth. I open and taste myself on his fingers, circling it as my body jolts from the aftershocks from my orgasm.

"Calm, Isa. Learn to control yourself, control your needs. Embrace what the fuck it feels like to be fucked, get fucked, and do the fucking. 'Cuz in here, baby, there are no. Limits." I want to blurt out how no limits is what turned me into a murderer, but I get the feeling right now isn't the time to be sassy.

I swallow, the taste of my arousal now clinging to the back of my throat. "Understood?" he demands my answer.

"Yes, understood."

"Good," he answers, his weight pressing down on me. Unlatching the handcuffs from their links, he presses the head of his cock to my entrance. "Leave the blindfold on until I say." He sinks into me, my pussy stretching to accommodate him as he circles and thrusts against me. Pulling out, he then dives back into me with a hiss escaping between his teeth. His hand flies up to my throat and clamps down on it so tightly, I will definitely pass out if he doesn't loosen it. Like my own personal collar.

"Holy shit." I let out a throaty groan, my head digging into the mattress from his weight pounding into me. He continues to ride my body expertly.

"You like that, baby. What do you want?"

"What?" I ask breathlessly, locked in my own world of pleasure.

"Tell me what you want, Isa, use your words."

"No, I can't use shit right now." What am I? A toddler.

He stops. His weight suddenly disappearing off of me causing the rude as fuck air to invade the space between our bodies.

"What are you doing!" I yell, reaching for the blindfold and ripping it off.

Bryant's shoulders straighten, his jaw clenches and his eyes remain dead as though they're peering straight through me. "I said use your words, Isa. Now..." he begins, walking back toward the bedside dresser slowly. He pulls it open and takes out a riding crop, the thick leather belts on either the end running over his olive skin as each muscle on his body flexes with fluid movements. "Tell me what you want, and I'll hit you once. Don't tell me what you want?" He grins, coming back toward the bed where I'm now crawling up like a scared little kitten. He takes hold of my ankles and drags me back down the bed until they're hanging off and my face is directly under his. Stepping between my legs, he places each fist on either side of my head and tilts his head. "You'll get two."

"Two?" Shit.

He nods, a dark smirk displaying across his face. "Yeah, babe, because either way, I'm getting your ass red tonight." It's as though he loves to inflict pain, like he almost needs to inflict pain to get off. It's hot, to a point. That point not being until I'm bleeding out on a bed, half fucked and half cut open, a dead man lying on top of me with a knife slit in his throat.

"I want..." I search for the right words. "I want you, inside me." Bryant flips me over until my stomach is pressing into the mattress.

"Not good enough, Isa. You can do better than that." With a loud slap, he belts down on my ass cheek and I screech out in pain, the shards of the sting pricking over the point of impact.

"Fuck!" I exclaim. "That hurts."

"Try again, Isa."

"I want your fucking tongue inside me until I come all over your face." I slam my mouth closed when I realize what I've said.

"Much fucking better." Gripping my hip bones, he yanks me up onto all fours, presses my head down into the mattress with his other hand and I feel the scruff of his beard brush over the flesh of my inner thighs. I pause, watching, waiting, until something or anything comes. His mouth covers my pussy from behind, his tongue flicking over my clit before dragging down, and in one push, it slips inside of me, circling my walls and hitting a spot deep inside perfectly.

"Yes," I groan, grinding against his mouth. His fingers

come up to my ass until he's pressing one inside roughly, pushing it deeper until his tongue is fucking me and his finger is smashing my ass. My orgasm tips over the edge from all the sensations that are engulfing me. He pulls back once I come down from my second orgasm and sinks back inside me, grabbing a fistful of my hair and tugging on it roughly until I feel the strands of my hair being torn out of their sockets. He slams into me relentlessly, as if he hates me and wants to kill me by shattering my cervix fucking open. His grip doesn't let up and I arch my back, feeling yet another orgasm build inside of me. A loud slap stings my left ass check as he continues to, pound into me. "Don't come."

"What!" I yell out through ragged breaths.

His cock pulses inside of me, throbbing against my walls and I collapse onto the bed like a starfish laying on my stomach. "Holy shit," I groan into the silk sheets, my body starting to pound with pain. With heavy eyes and sleep threatening to surface, Bryant flops down beside me and tosses the sheet over both of us. I don't move to accommodate him. I'm not moving for anyone.

He clears his throat. "I hate that I can't really blame you."

Before I can question what he means, I fall asleep.

7

What do you mean you're getting married?" Devon scoffs, following me around my room as I begin to gather all of my belongings. After leaving Bryant's place this morning, he told me to go home and pack a bag. I don't know what he expects me to do to be honest because those who know me know that I would never just pack up my life over a male.

"Yes, I am." I ignore his pleading stare and walk across the room and into the closet where I start taking clothes off the hooks.

"How the fuck can that happen?" Do I just tell him? He is my best friend. I've never hidden anything from him in my entire life. But if I tell him, I'd have to tell him the whole story—including me being a murderer. I'm not ready for my best friend to look at me as a murderer. I pause, clutching my bathrobe in my hand. I need to tell him something, though, or he won't believe me otherwise. Devon knows me. He knows that there's no way in hell I'd ever be on board to marry anyone let alone some hotshot I met after one night.

"Fuck." My hands falling in defeat before I turn to face him, my eyes coming to his worried ones. "You cannot say anything, Devon. This is serious and it involves a lot of people. Do you understand?"

"Goddammit, Isa!" He growls, walking toward me, every muscle on his chest flinching with his movements. He comes nose to nose with me, reaching up and clutching my face with his hands. Searching my eyes, he whispers, "I fucking love you, Isa. Tell me what's going on."

I exhale. "My dad, he, he sort of has to do with this. I'm... I *owe* him, and in order for me to get out of this rut he has put me in, I *must* marry Bryant Royal."

"—What rut? And—hold the fuck up!" He pauses, his face stilling and his hands dropping from my face. "Bryant Saint?" He looks back down at me, his eyes searching mine, waiting for me to answer.

"Yes..."

"No!" He shakes his head, stepping backward and tugging on his hair. "No, fuck that, Isa!"

"Fuck... what?" I reply, confused while matching his retreating steps. Dropping my robe to the ground, I slowly make my way toward him. "What does 'fuck that' mean?"

He drops down onto the bed, his hair still dripping wet from his shower, then he stares off blankly in front of himself. "Nothing."

"Right, okay, well now that you know, can you stop asking me questions?" I raise my eyebrows, about to throw out a sassy joke about how hot Bryant is when I see Devon's distressed stare. "Earth to Devon?" I wave my hand in front of him, but he still doesn't flinch.

"What?" he snaps, looking back toward me with a stare I have never seen from him before. Devon has been mad at me before, sure, what best friends don't have disagreements and all that, but this stare was something else. It was as if he hated me.

"I said now that you know, you can leave me alone about the subject?"

"Oh." Devon collects himself, smiling weakly. "Yeah, okay. I guess it makes more sense and all that."

"Good." I straighten my shoulders, surprised at how easy he was to convince. Even though I'm surprised, a huge relief has been lifted off my shoulders. "Now that that's settled, I'm leaving tonight."

There's a long pause. "Isa?" Devon groans, dropping his head to his hands and leaning over his elbows which are resting on his knees. "Please just tell me you will be careful."

I tilt my head. "Devon? What's wrong?"

He stands to his feet while shaking his head. "Nothing." Then he comes toward me, gripping the back of my neck and pulling my forehead to his lips. "Nothing at all," he whispers against my skin. Stepping back, he smiles weakly and I see a sad glint flash through his eyes. "I better go. I have a photoshoot thing at twelve, and the photographer hates when I'm late."

"Yeah." I walk toward my half-packed suitcase. "I'll see you a little later, or if I don't, I'll text you and we can grab some dinner or something?" I can't imagine my life without Devon in it. The thought not only cripples me but it—nope. I'm not going there.

He smiles again, stepping backward slowly. "Yeah, Just... text me." Then he's gone in a flash. Pausing for a split second, I think over at what point exactly, did that conversation go weird. I come up with nothing. Devon and I have always been close, so I can usually read him. The second we met each other we hit it off, and I knew instantly that we were going to be best friends, so him acting this way obviously is him being jealous about Bryant suddenly rail-roading my life. He's just being territorial.

Gathering up the last of my clothes, I head into the bath-room for all my toiletries and phone charger before slinging my backpack over my shoulder and wheeling my suitcase behind myself. I pause at the threshold of my room, turning around one last time. Last time? Maybe not. I don't plan to stay with Bryant for long. The second he's finished with whatever game he's playing, I'll be back. Switching off the light, I let that promise sink into an echo inside my brain...

FALLEN leaves crunch under my feet as I zip through the tree trunks and jump over old fallen branches. The air zips into my lungs like icicles from a cool winter day and the fog mists out of my mouth like smooth smoke from a cigar. Why am I running? Who am I running from? All I know is that I need to run. Jumping over a moss-covered log, I stop running, breathing in and out heavily. A wall of glass drops down in front of me, displaying my own reflection. It's peering back at me like an empty lost part of who I am. Cocking my head, I stare deep into my eyes, sinking into my own thoughts. My reflection stills and I step back, but my reflection remains the same, unmoving, frozen in time. Chills break out over my body as my eyes in the mirror begin to turn a light grey, dead, lifeless. Seconds pass before dark black lines begin to crack over my flesh in the mirror.

"Holy shit!" I gasp, stepping backward and covering my mouth with my hand. My chest starts to feel thick when suddenly I'm robbed of air. My throat feels as though a brick has been shoved inside of it, so I squeeze, hoping to rip out whatever it is that's stopping me from breathing. My face swells and veins pop out of my head. As I'm about to collapse to the ground, bats fly out of my mouth in a loud squeak just as the mirror bursts and

shards of the broken glass go flying over my skin, slicing me into pieces.

SWEAT DRIPS off my skin as I shoot up from the floor in a panic. What the fuck was that? Looking around the room, I notice I'm still in my apartment, my bedroom door slightly ajar. Rubbing my hands over my sweat-soaked flesh, a range of goosebumps break out all over me. I bend down, picking up my fallen handbag and suitcase. Whatever that was sent chills down my spine. Speeding up to a slight jog, I head toward the front door, pull it open and rush out the foyer until the cool breeze washes over my face. I don't know what the fuck that was. Too many weird things are going on in my life right now that I don't know how to comprehend them all at once. Devon going cold on me, Bryant being Wolf, and then whatever that dream was. Nothing's adding up and everything is starting to feel too overwhelming. "Isa!" Jerry runs up behind me with three other MIB's following closely.

"Sorry." I pause. "I swear," I look around nervously, my head still pounding, "I swear I wasn't trying to run."

Jerry looks at me closely, I see the way his eyes run over every inch of my body, checking to see that I'm not visibly hurt. Nope. Just a little fucking freaked out. "All right." Then he looks to another MIB. "Go and get the car." Before he takes hold of my arm and ushers me outside.

We're waiting for the car when my phone vibrates in my pocket, I quickly slip it out and answer.

"Hello?" I say breathlessly, moving my unruly dark hair out of my face and slipping into the backseat of the SUV.

"Isa? Have you been running, are you okay?" Step-mother dearest. I calm my breathing, closing my eyes. Of course she would think me running would be something totally out of the blue. I don't run, and if I am running, you should probably run too because that means something is chasing me.

"Yes, I'm fine, what can I do for you, Lydia?" We pull away from the curve after Jerry gets in beside me, and I crank down the window, attempting to dry off the excess sweat I still have trickling down the side of my face.

"Well... your father wanted to know how your night with Bryant Royal went..."

I scoff. Scoff. Flat out could not help the ridiculous scoff that escapes my mouth. "Oh, I'm sorry, so why didn't he call me himself?" I rest the phone on my shoulder and lean forward toward the driver. "Bryant's place, please." Then I lean back in my seat. "Tell him it was fine. Bryant and I have known each other for some time so we're picking up where we left off—why?" A terrible lie, but if my family isn't going to believe that I'm about to marry Bryant, it will only work if they think we've known each other for a while.

"Well..."

"Lydia, stop saying *well* and cut to the point."

"It's just... your father would really appreciate your cooperation in what Bryant may or may not ask you." I sigh, massaging my temples with my fingertips. Seems Bryant has already beaten me to it, though I should applaud him for his brilliant swerve in working my parents. Of course going this route would work better. This way it will make my father feel important.

Rolling my eyes, I tilt my head back into the headrest. "What exactly are you asking me?"

"Well, I think you know what it is that I'm asking you. Don't fight this, Isa. You could have done worse off. This is Bryant Royal for goodness sake." Having about enough of this conversation, I hang up my phone in a huff. Bryant has already interfered with so much in my life. I dial Devon's number, because, well, he's all I really have as far as friends go. Aside from Jen, but she's married with kids and will be jumping up and down to have me get with Bryant, so I could really do with Devon's insight in this situation. I know I can't disclose too many details to him right now, but he's always been good at talking me off the cliff. And I feel very close to falling off the cliff right now. Maybe he has cooled down enough to talk some sense into me.

After the fourth time of him not answering, I throw my phone onto the seat beside me and glance out the window to all the passing trees and runners jogging through the streets. The cute couple walking their fluffy Labrador and the mom who is pushing her stroller down the street as her child licks his half-melted ice cream. Why couldn't my life be this simple. As simple as strolling down the road on a relaxing Saturday morning? My life has never been simple or relaxing. Even when I was a little girl, Dad was non-existent, but yet somehow, he always managed to rule with an iron fist. My sister and I hardly had a life outside of our house and all though it didn't bother her so much, it sure as fuck bothered me.

We pull up to a stop outside of Peppers, where Bryant lives in his massive penthouse. Once I'm out of the car, Jerry already has my bags out from the trunk.

"Thanks, Jer."

He smiles, but it doesn't reach his eyes. Not that it does reach his eyes a lot, but I can sense something is stressing him, so I ask, "What's up, Jer?"

He cranks his neck and it looks like he's trying to relieve some of the tension from his neck. "We will be in the suite beside you. You need anything, you know I'm on speed-dial and of course, there will be someone outside your door at all times." I wanted to say how the one time I went back to this very place unprotected—probably my father's doing what with him all excited that I was about to bed Bryant— was the time I got semi-kidnapped. But I don't say that, of course, I just smile. "I know, Jer." Ending my sentence with a light pat on his shoulder. The doorman who guards Peppers is a little on the old side, and I could probably outrun him if I wanted—if I didn't hate cardio—but he seems nice enough.

Clearing my throat, I step forward and make my way toward the entrance. Walking through the glass doors, my phone vibrates in my pocket and I quickly shift hands to reach for it, excited that it might be Devon returning my call.

"Aw, you miss me and you're done being shitty?" I purr down the phone.

"Isa, the code to the penthouse is 4566." My smile drops instantly.

"Got it." Hanging up my phone, I shove it back into my pocket, this time a little more on the angry side. Bryant pisses me off, yes, but do we fuck like machines? Also yes. But I hate him. I hate him with a fire so hot it could burn the freaking sun. That was dramatic, but you catch my drift. Bypassing the reception desk, I head straight to the elevator and push the up button. Watching the numbers slowly drop has my stomach all twisted. Fuck. I'm doing this. I mean, I've already pretty much done it, but this time I'm really doing it. As in, I'm about to have all my shit in his apartment, and I can't go home.

This is fine, I can make it work. Bryant Royal doesn't scare me, no not at all. I'm Isa Johnson. A fucking badass who eats men like Bryant Royal for breakfast, lunch, dessert and still have room for a side dude. He has nothing on me.

Ding! The elevator doors slide open and I swallow past the ball of nerves that has set up in my throat. Fuck, I was thinking so much shit right then. I don't have myself at all.

Stepping inside, I watch as the doors slowly slide closed, and I try to allow the soft melody of music to calm my chaotic thoughts and raging feelings. I have no options right now. Whatever Bryant has on me is relevant to my surviving this ordeal—that much I do know. The car ascends higher, along with my gut until it comes to a halt and the doors slip open again, the familiar charcoal walls and the rich mahogany wood on display, yet again.

"Bryant?" I call out, walking into the apartment and removing my jacket. I know I should ask more questions about who it was that was there the day that he captured me. The day the truth came out. It feels like a lifetime away already, but I figure I already truly know who it was. It would have been one of the other guys from that day, whose faces I wouldn't be able to pick out if they were all lined up together. I didn't recognize Bryant as Wolf the first time I met him, there's no way I would notice the other guys. This is why drugs are bad and why you should stay in school.

"Yeah?" his voice cuts through my thoughts as he saunters into the kitchen. Dark loose sweatpants hang from his lean hips just as droplets of water drip off his floppy dark hair and cascade down over his chiseled chest.

Fuck me. This is not helping my train of thought at all. Then his ocean blue eyes pierce through me like lasers, so I quickly divert my eyes before I get sucked in.

With his eyes still on mine, he pulls open the fridge door and takes out a carton of milk, flicking it open before bringing it to his lips.

"Are you just going to stare or are you going to tell me a

plan?" I snap, tossing apartment keys onto the kitchen island.

He chuckles, swiping the milk from his lips. "You don't throw orders around, Isa. You will know the plan when I say you will know the plan. Until then, learn to control your mouth or I'll fuck the shit out of it. Are we clear?"

I grit my teeth. "Crystal." Not clear at all, but again, the play nice card. Which is going to be maxed out soon if he carries on like this. How long is he going to treat me like this? Because honestly, a girl can only take so much.

He points. "Go upstairs. I'll have someone collect the rest of your shit from your apartment." How he knew that I had left some of my belongings at my apartment, I don't know, so I follow his orders, heading up the stairs and into his room. I take a seat on the edge of his bed, just as he walks in moments later. He leans against the doorframe. "We have to lay the groundwork, and you won't make this difficult for me, Isa."

"I won't," I murmur, resting my elbows on top of my knees. "I just—what do you have on me and can I please see it?"

He glares at me, so I glare back. I don't back down without a cause, and him having a tape that could possibly prove I'm a murderer is a very good cause to back down for, but he's testing my self-control. Just when I think he's about to tell me to fuck off, he pushes off the wall and walks toward the closet that is opposite his bed. He disappears inside for a few seconds before coming back out, carrying a USB stick. Kneeling down, he reaches for a bag and places it on the bed, unzipping it but keeping his eyes on mine.

Pulling out a laptop, he throws the bag back onto the ground and takes a seat beside me, placing the laptop on his lap.

He looks at me. "You want to see or not?"

Kicking off my shoes, I crawl down the bed and sit just behind him, enough that I can see the screen of the laptop clearly.

He chuckles, shakes his head, and then looks back to the screen, hitting play on a video. I see from the corner of the room where I walk in. It was just after Brooke and I—well, Brooke—hit some lines of coke, and the four post bed is in clear view of the camera. Bile rises in my throat and I close my eyes, trying to squash down the memories. Seeing the tent again isn't something I thought through—obviously. I know what happens about five minutes after that and so on. It's obvious that they recorded the whole thing. "I don't need to see anymore."

He shuts the laptop and turns to face me. "We could both benefit from this, Isa. It gets your dad off your case, too."

I can't help but laugh, sliding off the bed. "Who said my dad was an issue for me?"

He shrugs. "The fact that at almost every social event, you hated it, but yet you were obligated to go."

I pause. Honestly quite shocked at his answer. I thought my fake smile was on point. "How would you know?"

He halts, looking up at me from picking up his bag, then grins. "I'm observant."

Brushing my hair out of my face, I stand and place my hands on my hips. "Okay so what exactly are you proposing? What's the plan?"

He gets to his feet and struts right up to me. Cocking his head, his eyes scan over my face. "Business arrangement. You stay here, play wife to what everyone out there," he points to the windows, "thinks, but in short, we remain *open.*"

Okay, see this was what I was afraid of.

"Hang on a second…" I interject, trying my hardest not to bite his fucking dick off. "So what you're basically saying is that I will have to be okay with you sleeping with other people?"

He quirks an eyebrow. "Tell me, who have I ever been known to sleep with?"

"What, media-wise?" I ask, tilting my head and wondering where in the hell he is going with this.

He nods, a small grin coming on display. "Yes, media-wise."

I think over what he's just asked. As far as the research I've done goes, he hasn't been known to be with anyone. If I looked hard enough, though, or if Devon looked hard enough (because that man should be in the CIA), I bet we could find something. And anyway, what has that got to do with anything. "No, but what has that got to do with my question?"

"Answer me this honestly, Isa." His chest brushes against mine. "If you had the chance to get fucked, any which way you wanted, and it not be leaked online, would you do it? Hmm?" he asks, running his eyes up and down my body.

"Well, yeah. But because of my dad, I never get that option so I settle on one-night stands or…" I pause, and then my mouth snaps shut.

"Or Devon," Bryant continues for me anyway.

My eyes slant. "How do you know about Devon?"

His face turns to stone, and then he barges past me, heading toward the bathroom. "I know everything there is to know about you, Isa. Get changed, we need to start on our groundwork."

I GOT CHANGED in record time, mostly because Bryant was waiting for me in the sitting room, and what I guess, glaring at his watch every second. He wants us to start working on our 'groundwork,' whatever the fuck that means. Slipping on my strappy shoes, I take one last glance in the mirror. Well, this is more than over the top for groundwork. What if said groundwork is covered in mud, then this Louis Vuitton beige strapless short dress will no doubt get ruined. I wouldn't even flinch, I hope it pains him. Although guessing from the amount of money Bryant has, I don't think he'd care—no scratch that, I know that he wouldn't care.

"You done?" he asks from the doorway. I look at him in the mirror, admiring what he's wearing. Well, damn, it doesn't matter how many times I've seen Bryant in a suit, every time I see him in one my mouth waters the same.

"Yup!" I cut off my own thoughts, picking up my clutch from my bed and wrapping the chain around my fist. I'm going to need to go and buy a vibrator because this lack of sex thing is not working for me.

We both get into the Ferrari once we reach the parking lot, and I take a look at the side mirror while reaching for my safety belt, watching as Jerry and three other MIB's get into the black Range Rover behind us. Bryant puts the gear into reverse. "So," I start, looking toward him. "What are we doing to start this groundwork?"

"Work party."

"Figures," I mutter, looking out the window as he floors it out from the underground parking and onto the busy street.

On our way to wherever this work function is, I created a plan. Bryant isn't making this easy for me. In fact, he's making it very difficult with his asshole tendencies. If he were nicer, maybe I would have come to him on my own accord instead of him basically blackmailing me into marrying him.

That's a lie and I know it. I just maybe wouldn't have thought of this plan that I'm thinking about right now.

1) I can't just accept this fate. But if I do anything, will he unleash the tape to the police? He could.

2) He wouldn't. He's already expressed how much he wants and needs me to be his wife, therefore, I'm far more useful to him when I'm not behind bars.

Which leads me to 3) What have I always been good at when I'm not getting caught attempting to do it—which technically, makes me pretty shit at it—Run.

We pull up to the front of a huge glass building. The front of the doors have 'Royal Enterprise Holdings' sprawled out in grey lettering, and look, there's even a gold crown as the company logo. How poetic. Rolling my eyes, I get out of the car and shut the door behind myself. In order for my plan to work, it will need to happen tonight, because the longer I leave it, the harder it will be for me to leave. I don't want to give Bryant any time to sweet talk me into convincing myself that he's not a bad person because he is. Bad for me, at least. Jerry and the three MIB's get out of the Range Rover and walk up to us. "It's all secure. I had some eyes look around the premise before we got here."

Bryant looks to Jerry. "I wouldn't bring her here if it weren't secure, and this is my kingdom." He pauses, narrowing his eyes onto Jerry. This could go one or two different ways. I'm really hoping it heads toward the way I need, because I couldn't deal with the two men whom I spend most of my time with fighting at my every turn. "But I appreciate you looking out." I let out a long, but silent exhale.

Bryant gestures to the front doors. "Shall we?"

I fight an eye roll to show my enthusiasm. This better not be a long night.

THE MILKY SOAP suds drip off my body as the steam from the shower fogs the glass. I've been in here for ten minutes. I'm usually a long shower person so it won't be out of the ordinary for Bryant, not that we've been together long enough for him to make any sort of assumptions in regards to shower time. For all he knows, I'm a quick shower taker. Or maybe, I'm one of those people who sometimes has a quick shower, or sometimes has a long shower. Regardless, I'm in here. With my passport and credit card hidden under my towel that's sitting on the bathroom counter, so far, my plan is going well. Now, all I have to do is get out of this apartment without waking Bryant or by alerting Jerry next door. Admittedly, Jerry and the MIB's have laid back a lot since we've been here, probably because of their knowledge of Bryant. Hitting the faucet on the shower, I get out, wrapping the towel around me. Drying up in record time, I stop all movements. What is the possibility of Bryant trying to fuck with me tonight?—bang.

"Isa!"

Shit. Shit.

I silently clear my throat. "Won't be long."

Maybe I shouldn't have said that. My tone was a little too cheerful. Usually, I probably would have told him to fucking wait.

"I'm going for a run."

My eyes almost pop out of their sockets, I'm that shocked at how perfect his timing is. I can't act happy though, I need to be careful. Be Isa.

"Sure thing!" I call out, and then it's silent.

My paranoia begins to eat at the surface of my fears, so if I'm doing this, it needs to happen now. I won't get this prime opportunity again.

Slipping into my nightie like I had planned, I shove my passport and Visa into the side of my G-string and then fluff my nightie back over it. Running a brush through my hair, I tie it into a high messy bun before yanking the door open. Pausing in the doorway, I listen for any clues or sounds. Satisfied with the fact that Bryant has gone, I walk out with a smirk on my face. I'm about to be free, free as a bird—A hand flies to my throat and clenches tightly, shoving me up against the wall.

8

Gasping for air, I tap at Bryant's hand, but he doesn't budge. The room is dark, silent and eerie, and all I can hear is Bryant's deep inhale of breaths.

He squeezes tightly again, then growls over my neck, "Give me three reasons why I shouldn't kill you." He eases his grip, just enough to allow some air. "You have ten seconds."

"Ah," I begin after a quick throat clear.

"Ten." His knee comes between my legs, spreading them apart.

"You'd have to dispose of my body."

"I own a pig farm. Seven."

Fuck! Wait, does he really own a pig farm? "—six." His thigh presses hard against me. Focus. "You like my dad."

"I'd like you dead more." He cups my breast with one hand and squeezes while bringing his lips to the center of my neck. "Four," he whispers against my skin. I swallow.

Fuck. Think, Isa. Think. "Because I promise I'll play wife for you and do as you want."

I feel his grin spread out over my skin and I quite honestly have to fight the urge to knee him in the nuts. He bites my neck. "Get on your knees."

I do as I'm told, dropping to my knees in front of him. He wraps my hair around his fist before yanking my head back so I'm looking up at him. Completely submissive, and whole-heartedly his toy. "Remove your clothes." Again, I do as I'm told. Pulling at the sash that was tied tightly around my waist. Keeping my eyes on his, I feel the silk unlatch from my body and drop to a heap around my knees. Now I'm in nothing but my G-string with my passport and visa tucked into the sides.

Oopsie.

His eyes drop to the passport before he grips both items and throws them across the room. "You try that shit again, and I'll kill you."

9

D eep breaths, Isa. It's going to be fine," Lydia coos, fluffing over my dress. She's so fucking wrong that it's almost funny. Almost because I don't find it amusing at all. Since moving in with Bryant, everything has been at full speed. Hard to believe that it was just a week ago when I got caught attempting to run. Yeah, that turned out really great. The only running I have done was the running of a cold bath after he spanked my ass so hard I couldn't sit down for days.

"It's not going to be okay, Lydia, because I don't want to get fucking married." I've never been very good at hiding my thoughts to Lydia. As much as she drives me nuts, there are parts of me that respects her too. I mean, she tolerates my father.

"Oh, sweetness." Lydia pats my cheek, her cool leather-like palm skating over my plush cheek. "Marriage is over-rated. You could have been worse off. Count your lucky stars."

I pause. Over the years, I've known Lydia to take little jabs at her and Dad's marriage. I don't know their story or why they're together, but I've known for some time that Lydia wasn't happy. I mean, all you need to do is take one look at her and it's obvious.

"Lydia?" I ask, straightening my dress while looking at myself in the mirror and tilting my head. "If you're not happy with Dad, why don't you leave?" She seems to ponder over my question until a few silent beats passing us.

"Sometimes we do things because we have to, Isa. Not because we want to." There's that connection. This is why, because I know that underneath that strong shell, she hides a lot of pain. Pain that maybe I won't understand just yet, but I hope to in the future.

Breathing in and out deeply, and hearing her passive aggressive comment loud and clear, I exhale. "Okay."

Pulling open the door to the master bedroom of Bryant's apartment, I gather the train of my dress, lifting it up off the floor. "Deep breathing," I whisper to myself in hopes to calm down. Lydia steps in front of me, taking the lead and I follow, walking toward the elevators. Once inside, we descend down a level, the doors opening to Jerry and around six MIB's. Must be added security because of the day and all. I mean, I'm about to marry my worst enemy, I'm pretty sure the only threat to my life is from my husband-to-be.

"You look beautiful, Mrs. Johnson." Jerry nods his head toward me. Something warm blossoms deep inside my chest and I smile sweetly at him. "Thanks, Jer." The elevator continues down until eventually, we're in the lobby, heading toward a large white stretch limo that's sitting outside. I bypass all the stares that I'm getting out of the corner of my eyes, and walk through the front doors, out toward the awaiting car. The driver jumps out, popping open the back door, just as Jerry and the MIB's pile into a couple SUV's. One is in front of us and another behind us.

"Thank you." I smile at our driver, sliding into the backseat as quickly as I can with Lydia climbing in behind me.

"Wait!" Brianna yells, coming down toward the limo. "Sorry I'm late," she adds, slipping into the backseat and sitting opposite me. Typical Brianna fashion.

"Thanks for showing," I sarcastically add, closing the door and leaning my head against the cool window. My idea of having a relaxing trip is now ruined, thanks to my sister. So much for 'I'll meet you all down there.'

"Are you mad?" Brianna asks, putting her earrings into her ears. "You know that I had a conference today, Isa. I made do the best I could and I mean, hey! I'm still here aren't I? Even if I am missing my shoes, and in my defense, I had short notice to attend. I would have liked to lose a couple pounds—if you know what I mean." No, I don't, because my sister is a size freaking two.

"Oh, for fuck's sake!" I shake my head, choosing which part of her sentence I want to reply to. "How'd you manage to lose your shoe?" I chose the easiest one.

Brianna shrugs. "I'm me, that's how." She's right, no explanation needed. As put together my sister is on the outside, she's a klutz. A natural fucking disaster waiting to happen. The only difference between her and I is that she hides her category 5 cyclone ass better than I can. Even when we were kids, Brianna would be next to me through everything. She may appear to be perfect and well-polished, but she's always been loyal to me, even when we were kids. I'd be getting into trouble, but she'd always be there in an attempt to save me. She always tried to butter our father up to go easy on me, but he never did.

"Isa," she whispers, finally finished with her shoe and leaning over, flicking open the little bar fridge. She takes out the chilled bottle of champagne and two flutes before leaning back into her seat. I try to ignore her penetrating glare and look out the window, watching the passing trees whisk past as we head toward the Chapel in downtown New York City.

"Isa?" Brianna repeats. I can see her trying to hand me my flute of champagne, so I take it, but keep my eyes locked on the passing world.

"What?" I answer softly, bringing the rim of my glass to my mouth and taking a sip.

"Is everything okay? Did Dad have something to do with this marriage?" she pries, leaning forward.

I swallow the bitter bubbles and shake my head. "No, Brianna. This is my doing—for once," I lie. I hate lying to her, and usually, it's useless because she always could tell when I was bullshitting, but because I have so much at stake here, I'm going to put on an Oscar-worthy performance.

"So Dad had absolutely nothing to do with this?" she repeats, her undertone saying she doesn't believe a word I'm saying, as she throws herself back into her seat. Glaring at her as she takes a long pull of the champagne, I snap, just as she swallows. "So what if he did, Bri, what am I supposed to do about it? What have we *ever* been able to do about it?" So much for Oscar-worthy performance. That was terrible.

"Jesus." Briana leans forward again, her soft chocolate eyes coming to mine. "*He* does doesn't he?" She shakes her head, then leans closer. "This is marriage, Isa. This is a contract, binding your soul to someone else."

I chuckle, taking another sip of my crisp champagne which is going down rather nicely. "Stop being so dramatic.

It's only soul binding if you're in love with said person—which I'm not."

"God!" she curses. "That's even fucking worse!"

"How so?" I tilt my head. "The way I see it; I'll never get hurt. Fuck love."

"Isa…"

"Shut up, Bri." I look back at her. "Okay? Just… *shut up*."

"Okay. But answer one thing and answer it truthfully."

I roll my eyes. "What?"

"Has this got anything to do with Brooke?"

…

"Are you fucking kidding me, Brooke!" I laughed, the effects of the alcohol swimming through my veins and warming my blood.

"I'm dead serious!" Brooke giggled, taking my hand in hers. "Come, let's just do it for fun!"

"Fun?" I yanked my hand back.

"It's a strip club, Isa! They'll give us a job straight away and this way, we can make money doing something we're good at!"

"You can, I'm not into the whole stripping thing…"

She winked at me. "Well, you can get drunk and watch me do the whole stripping thing, huh? How about that?" Mmm. She had a point.

"That sounds like a better plan." I smirked at her, nudging my head toward the glass opening doors.

She hooked her arm in mine, then pushed open the door. I glanced around the dim setting, watching as the strobe lights flashed and the deep bass of some rock song electrified the atmosphere.

"Wait at the bar!" Brooke yelled into my ear over the music and I nodded, walking toward one of the leather bar stools.

"What can I get you?" The bartender asked me, but my eyes were still glued on Brooke and her retreating frame. It wasn't until she slipped behind the stage curtain that I turned to face the bartender.

"Hi, ah, anything with vodka in it. Thanks." His greying beard trailed down his chest, but not in a greasy way, more in a slick, silver fox way. His eyes were silver and his hair was styled back tidily. He must've been in his sixties? Or maybe late fifties, but he was handsome for an old guy, to say the least.

"Coming up, darlin'," he winked, moving to the other side of the bar and pulling out a few more glasses. "You from around here?" He placed the glasses down and took out a bottle of vodka.

I shook my head. "No. Me and my friend are just passing through."

"And this friend..." he asked, watching me skeptically while pouring our drinks. "She's stripping while you pass through?"

I laughed, taking the glass from him. "Yeah, well we're sort of just drifting through while we figure out what college we want to go to. Or if we even want to go to college."

"Huh," he murmured, tilting his head. "That's interesting."

"Not really," I muttered back, swallowing my drink. I looked around the room again, noticing that there were only a few people scattered around the place. "Is it usually this quiet?"

The bartender dragged his eyes over my seated frame and then shook his head. "Not usually. But it's Wednesday, that means that it's private events only – usually."

"Oh!" I straightened in my seat. "Are we not supposed to be here?"

He paused, the wrinkles around the corner of his eyes crinkling, illustrating his age. "Naaw, darlin', you're good." I thank him and then turn in my chair, just in time to see Brooke sauntering down the catwalk stage to "Killing Strangers" by Marilyn Manson.

My head was a little hazy from my drink, and the lack of food throughout the day probably didn't help, but I continued to watch as Brooke slowly wrapped her body around the beat of the song and all eyes in the room shot straight to her. I smirked, knowing full well what she was doing. Aside from being seductive and sultry, Brooke was the most exotic girl I had ever seen. With chocolate brown wavy hair, bright blue eyes, a tight body, and a tan most girls would die for, she was gorgeous. She looked toward me, body rolling against the poll and come-hithered her fingers. I was about to shake my head when the buzz from the alcohol shot straight to my brain and relaxed my frantic thoughts. I grinned, sliding off my stool and walked toward the front of the stage.

"Get it, darlin'," one of the guys at the tables in front of us catcalled.

Looking over my shoulder at him, I winked and snatched the joint he had pressed to his lips, bringing it to my own. I took a long inhale of the harsh smoke, removing my leather jacket and tossing it across the room before blowing out a thick white cloud. Taking off my shirt, I popped the button off my jeans and shimmied out of them slowly, a smirk riding on my lips. Placing the joint back in my mouth, I kicked my jeans to the side and slid my butt up onto the stage. Smiling at the young guys in the front dressed in suits, I flicked the joint back toward them, the ash erupting over the impact of it hitting him, before gripping onto the pole and winging it. Whatever I remember watching on TV as a kid when it came to dancing, I used this night. In my drunken, stoned haze, nothing mattered. But truly, nothing mattered since that night in the tent. Somehow, all of that had made me numb. Taking someone's life wasn't something to be proud of, but when a man doesn't know how to take no for an answer, whether it's his kink or not, then he deserved what he got.

At least, that's what I tell myself when it begins to be too much. Since then, living life in the fast lane with Brooke, a bottle of whiskey, a few lines of coke, and a strip club, seemed like the more pleasurable route to my destruction.

Brooke removed her bra and flung it across the room toward an older guy that had been looking at her like she was a big juicy steak and he was starved. She made her way down to him, jumping off the stage while still moving to the music. Wrapping her legs around his lap, she started grinding against him. I chanced a look at his friend beside him just as his eyes connected with mine. He nudged his head, pulling out hundred-dollar bills from his pocket. Smirking, I leaped down off the stage, turned my back toward him, and ground my ass into his lap.

"Hey, baby, wanna let me have a touch and I'll triple your tips?" He groaned hoarsely into the side of my neck. He smelled of stale beer and cheap cigarettes.

"Triple, huh? And touch where?" I spun around, wrapped my legs around his waist and took a seat on his lap, grinding myself over the bulge that was coming through the front of his pants. Money, think money. My head was drifting around to the music when a dark shadowed figure caught my attention. I couldn't see from where I was what it was because not only was this object in the shadows, but their face was covered by a long hoodie. There's one thing I did know, though. Based on the structure of the figure and the long hair, it was definitely female.

Bringing my attention back to the task at hand, he smiled, the wrinkles on his face curving around his teeth. "Anywhere I want." He grabbed one of my tits and squeezed through my bra. I didn't mind. After all, we needed the money. After I left home, my dad and Lydia disowned me. They never understood Brooke, but they never understood many people. If you couldn't serve a purpose to my father or my family, then there's no way they'd make time for you. Brooke had nothing to offer, and I figured that's why they always had a very distasteful opinion on her.

I first met Brooke one night when I almost crashed my car into the town's bridge. I skidded to a halt, tears streaming down my face, in full panic mode because I was drunk and was also hell-bent on thinking someone was following me. Brooke had said there was no one following me, so I eventually calmed down. I put it down to all my emotions running high from catching my then-boyfriend cheating on me at the party I had just come from, and the alcohol running through my system. Brooke had showed up as I was having a full-blown panic attack in my car that was up on the footpath to the bridge. I've often wondered why my family don't speak to her or even acknowledged her when she was around, and I've always thought that maybe they assumed we dated because of how Brooke was and how close our friendship was. Wrong. Brooke and I enjoy dick too much to switch teams, but we're comfortable enough around each other to experiment with other people together.

I ran my hands down the old dude's sides until they stopped at a cold metal barrel. "Oh?" I smiled, attention perked.

"Just protection, darlin', nothing to worry your pretty little self about."

I go to reach for the gun but he stopped me with a firm grip of his hand. "Pretty little girls shouldn't play with big ugly guns."

"Aw, that's cute." I winked at him, letting it go. NERD "Lapdance" came on so I continued giving the man his excitement while letting his fingers roam where ever they may—which occasionally ended in him shoving Benjamin Franklin's down the front of my bra—I laughed, hooking my fingers behind his neck and swinging myself backward.

Looking to the side, I watched as Brooke bent over between the guy who she was with legs, lean forward, and snort a line of crank off the inside of his thigh. In one quick motion, she then *flicked her wrist from behind her back and quickly pulled out a Swiss army knife. The room started spinning and I tilted my head just as she raised the knife to the man's throat, slicing deep across his jugular vein and blood started spurting out everywhere. The man I was sitting on, pounced off his seat, reaching for his semi-automatic, but I was faster. Snatching it quickly, I raised it up to him and cocked it. "Don't fucking move!"*

Brooke stood over the dead man's body, her breathing heavy, her chest rising and falling and blood dripping off her silken skin.

"Brooke?" I whispered out urgently, not knowing what the fuck just happened or what my next move should be. "What the fuck is going on?" Brooke looked over her shoulder to the young guys who were seated at the front of the stage and then flicked her gaze to the old man behind the bar. I kept my sole focus on the guy in front of me, though, not wanting to give him the opportunity to see a weakness. Never held a gun in my entire life, so I was totally winging this whole ordeal, but I was going with it. "Brooke!" I snapped at her.

"Honey, put the gun down. He ain't got shit he can do." The old guy from the bar walked toward Brooke and I, but I didn't lower the weapon. My hands shook, and my lips trembled slightly, but I remained in the same position.

"Isa, lower the gun," Brooke answered softly, reaching into the pockets of the dead guy and taking out all his money, shoving it into her pocket.

"Someone needs to tell me what the fuck is going on and they need to tell me right now! Or I'm not lowering shit." My breathing was ragged and all senses had been tightened by the adrenaline.

Old guy from the bar pulled out a seat opposite me, putting a cigarette between his lips. "Brooke?" he questioned, and then his eyes moved to the corner where the shadow once stood. His eyes changed, then he grinned, with a shrug of his shoulders. "That man there," he pointed down to the dead body on the floor. "Had been raping Brooke." He stopped, his left eye slightly twitching. I looked back to the man who was standing in front of me, afraid that he may jump on me, or hell, kill me. "Since she was a little girl." He flicked open his Zippo and took a long inhale of the nicotine. "Brooke?" He blew out a cloud of smoke. "She's my daughter, but her mother was seeing two people at the same time. Long story short, she was raised here and not... by me."

"But..." I whispered. "I never knew..." That was the best I could muster at this time.

"Give me the gun, darlin', and walk out of here." I looked to Brooke and she smiled softly, nodding her head. I flung the gun toward him and he swung it around his finger until the barrel was resting on his shoulder. He pulled the trigger and the other Russian—or English man— who I had at gunpoint, dropped to the ground in a bloody mess.

"I'll call you, Dad," Brooke muttered softly.

"You call me, darlin', you know where I am."

I looked at the other two guys who were sitting at the front of the stage, both had to be in their mid-twenties. Cocking my head, one of them grinned at me, his white teeth coming into display devilishly.

"Come on" Brooke interrupted my staring, so I followed her, picking up my clothes on the way out all the while feeling both of the young guy's glare at the back of my head. Once we had our clothes, I looked at Brooke just before we hit the front doors. "Who are those guys and why didn't you tell me this was your plan all along?"

"Those guys are my dad's minions." She didn't stop walking.

"Brooke!" I yelled out to her, gripping onto her arm as she made her way toward the car. She stopped and turned to face me. "And who is your dad? And who is your mom?"

She smiled weakly. "He owns a cartel that runs most of the

eastern side of America, and my mom? She..." Her eyes drifted off
into the distance sadly. "She's difficult." Then she walked back to
her side of the car with a complete smile back on her face. "You
ready to continue our road trip of mass destruction?"

"Yeah." I shook my head, attempting to wrap my head around
everything I just witnessed. "Yeah, but no more killing people.
We're going to be leaving a trail in our wake soon."

Brooke laughed, sliding into the driver's seat. "Promise, no
more dead bodies."

BRINGING myself out of my memory lapse, I look toward my
sister and smile. "No. Nothing to do with Brooke."

"Are you sure?" Brianna asks, doing that annoying thing
with her eyebrow when she knows I'm lying.

"Positive. Now can I just get this wedding over with,
please? I feel like my life hasn't even started yet but I'm over
it already." I sink back into my chair.

WE PULL up to a white chapel, and I note how it looks
exactly as it did in the brochures. I didn't get much time to
plan, and it didn't mean that great of a deal to me at the
time, so it was merely me choosing out of the eight venues
the wedding planner picked out for me.

Jen is waiting for me at the curb in her bridesmaid's
dress, and seeing her should make me happy, but it makes
me sad. Sad because I still haven't heard from Devon, and
I've become so lost without him. I've never thought of
myself to rely on anyone in my entire life, not my father or
my sister, but without even realizing, I did rely on Devon.
Emotionally, sexually, and just as a friend in general. One

thing I have learned through this rough patch is that friends can break your heart just like any relationship can.

Jen opens my door and widens her arms. "Oh my God, Isa, you look so stunning." I get out of the car with Brianna holding my train behind me. I feel terrible because amongst all the chaos that has happened in my life, I've lost touch with Jen. It's as though we both just took different paths in life, hers being having kids and marrying her high school sweetheart at a young age, and me, well, me being the hot mess that I am. Somehow, even though we love each other dearly, those little differences in life can be big things when it comes to friendship.

"Can you get out? I don't want to be stuck in here all day," Lydia mutters impatiently from inside the limo.

I pull Jen into a hug, and then step back. "You look beautiful too, Jen, Brianna did really well with your guy's dresses." I gave Brianna three options to choose from in regards to the bridesmaid dresses, and what did she do? She chose one thing of each option and then customized it. Andrea, the wedding planner, was not a fan of Bri.

"Thank you. My kids are probably running circles around David right now." She looks toward the church, and we both giggle. She's right, all though I do love her two kids very much, they're little mini tornados.

"Okay, are we ready?" Brianna grins, brushing her own dress down.

Jen smiles before nodding. "As ready as we will ever be."

The white doors spread open and I step inside just as our guests get to their feet. This whole thing is like a car wreck of a movie. I feel like a fraud, standing at where the aisle begins. Every step I take down the long wooden pathway, one hundred things rush through my brain—all of which have a lot to do with running. But considering my track record with running, I'm thinking I better not.

Looking up, I slowly bring my eyes to the altar, and they don't flinch away from Bryant. I know he has two men as his groomsmen, probably guys from that day—probably the same guys that helped practically kidnap me when I was in his house, or maybe, they're paid actors. The latter makes a lot of sense, and both options aren't very romantic. Figures. Good thing I'm not a scrapbook wedding enthusiast because this would absolutely shit on any and all expectations.

Bryant is dressed in a razor-sharp, perfectly tailored suit. The little black bow tie that is hooked around his neck catches my eye, mainly because I've never seen him in a bowtie, he's almost always wearing a tie. I bring my eyes back to his and I watch as he runs his own down my body, slowly. Yet, even though this is my wedding day, and although I know that it's not the traditional wedding—not even remotely, a part of me does feel a tinge of guilt, or discomfort, knowing how fake the whole set up is. But as Bryant takes my hand with a cocky grin, I notice something. On my side of the church sits Lydia, my father, a couple of my aunts whom I haven't seen in years, my cousin Trish— who is a nutcase—her husband and three kids, and a few distant cousins, but when I look to Bryant's side, it's full. Way fuller than my side. I didn't realize it, but he has a massive family. I don't know what I was expecting, actually, no, I know that I was expecting a lot smaller. Not saying people with smaller families are snobbish, but Bryant just comes off as someone who wouldn't have a large family. I'm guessing the woman standing at the front with a wide smile on her face is his mom. She has soft brown curls, warm chocolate eyes and a smile that could light up this entire church.

Bryant narrows his eyes on me, interrupting my gawking. "What's wrong?"

I perch my eyebrow. "Want the list?"

Bryant chuckles then looks back toward the priest. "Begin."

10

"Get in the car, Isa,"

Bryant growls into my ear while his hand is pressed firmly against my lower back.

I smile my 'smile' and give one last polite wave to our family and friends before gripping my dress in the palm of my hand and slipping into the backseat of the limo. Bryant's family was normal which surprised me. I didn't quite expect his mom to be so.... Motherly? I don't know, but a man like Bryant just screamed to me mommy issues, so that left me with thoughts of his father, but was proven wrong there too. His father, all though he seemed rather brooding, was in my opinion, normal. Everything about his damn family was normal and just... nice. My family and their rich ass friends were always such assholes to other people. I always thought it was money that made people assholes, but nope. Bryant's parents sure shat on that theory.

My smile drops as soon as I'm in the enclosure of the limo. I reach for the unopened bottle of champagne, unwrapping the cork and quickly popping it off. Without seeking out any wine glasses, I bring the rim of the bottle to my mouth and pound it back, letting the bitter rich liquid bubble down my throat. In the corner of my eye, I see Bryant slide into the chair opposite me, but I keep drinking.

I'm a wife.

A. Fucking. Wife.

I feel like I should be wearing a "ain't no wifey" shirt right now. I'm not fucking wife material, I'm life-changer, will-fuck-your-world-up, bitch-with-problems, material.

Bryant chuckles, slamming the door closed and that's when I lower my lovely bottle of champ while wiping my mouth with the back of my hand. All class, obviously. Hashtag classy wifey.

"What!" I snap at him, raising the bottle once more to take a drink.

"I didn't say anything, *wife*," he snarls. The pet name sets off goosebumps, or pissed off bumps, over my flesh. What the actual fuck have I done? I've made a lot of very questionable decisions in all my twenty years, but this...oh this has got to take the crack cake.

"Easy on the wife," I add, as the limo drives away from our guests.

"I'll call you what I want, but for the record, that's exactly what the fuck you are." He loosens his tie and tosses it across the seat. His dark eyes come to mine, and I take this time to scan his features, what with the soft lighting in the limo casting shadows over his chiseled jaw. There's no denying how stunning Bryant Royal is. No questioning at all. But then again, that's never been the issue.

"Why me?" I ask, you know, classic me, spitting out whatever is on my mind before I can throw up any kind of filter. "I mean," I rest the bottle of champagne between my thighs, "I mean, just why me?"

He pauses, and my eyes come to where his index finger

is working his upper lip. Just when I'm about to tap out and look away from his annoyingly sexy glare, he answers. "Would you believe me if I said I don't know?"

"No." I want to scoff, but I can't find the will to do it. It's somewhere between all the tension that has heightened to dangerous levels, and the urge to punch him square in the nose.

He exhales, reaching forward and taking the bottle from between my legs. "Good. At least you have something switched on in that brain."

"Not funny." I throw back at him, my eyes narrowed.

"I'm not trying to be funny, Isa." He takes a large gulp of champagne, his Adam's apple bobbing past his swallow.

"Well then what, Bryant. I know what I did to your brother... but why would you want to marry someone who took someone so close to you?"

He stops, his eyes snap straight to mine and if I didn't know any better by knowing that it wasn't (actually) possible, I'd say flames roared inside those dark pupils. "Why the fuck do you have to ask so many questions?" He tilts his head and runs his eyes over my body. "For someone who didn't ask fuck all questions when she was supposed to, you sure ask a lot now."

"That's not fair," I flinch, mumbling it more to myself than to him because truly, someone like Bryant doesn't give a flying fuck about what I think is fair.

"A lot of shit isn't fair," *ding, ding, ding, maybe I should have been a psychic*, "but you being incapable of asking questions is not one of them." Oh, we're definitely going to kill each other before we've even reached the boring phase of marriage.

Deciding to ignore him for the rest of the trip, I lean my head against the cool window and watch the passing of trees. All these recent events have had me thinking about Brooke a lot. I think she's with her dad somewhere, I haven't heard from her in some time.

Looking to Bryant out of the corner of my eye, I want to ask him what we're doing. What his plan is and why he had to marry me. Aside from being the president's daughter, and having history with his brother, I don't see why he would (truly) benefit from having me as his wife.

Pulling into the underground parking lot, we get out of the limo and I clutch my dress in my hand. This isn't as I imagined I spend the night of my wedding, not that I thought about it much, but still, I watch movies, and this isn't usually how it plays out, but then again, nothing ever is.

Going back into the penthouse, I toss my phone onto the counter and head straight for the fridge. Taking out the only champagne bottle I see in there, I rip the cork off and bring it to my lips. I hear Bryant snicker behind me. "You know I have glasses, right?"

Swallowing the bubbles, I turn to face him while letting my hair down. "You know it's our wedding night, right?"

His mouth snaps closed as his eyes darkened. "Don't ask for something you ain't ready for, Isa."

"Mmmm." I inch my finger up. "And who says that I'm not ready? Sex, yes, Marriage, no."

Bryant comes closer, so I step backward until I'm colliding with the fridge doors. Once he's close, he brings both fists up to my head and cages me in. He tilts his head, running his tongue over his teeth before his lip curls up. "Take off your dress," he growls, so deep that it awakens that same dark little girl who shamelessly begs for Bryant every day. Every night. Every time he flashes those annoying fucking eyes toward me, she stirs deep inside me begging to be fucked—hard. Instantly, my fingers find the back of my dress until I'm slowly zipping it down. Bryant's head drops down as he watches my flesh slowly be revealed to him. He steps backward, reaching for the bottle of champagne from my other hand, and then bringing it to his mouth. He takes a long pull of it, but his eyes remain on mine. Just as the tight silk drops off my skin and the fresh air pinches my nipples, a growl comes from his chest.

Yikes! The no bra idea was obviously a great idea. Leaning against the fridge, I smile at him, hooking my G-string and tugging it off. Swinging it around with my index finger, I reach out to Bryant, a slight smile on my mouth. "Is this what you want?" I close my eyes, my hips beginning to roll at the thought of Bryant right there, watching me. I don't know why, but he sets my *everything* on fire. The erotic feeling engulfs me, and I get lost in it.

When he doesn't answer, I carry on. "Is it?" My eyes are closed as my fingers involuntarily find my clit. "To see, smell, taste what you do to me?"

A hand clenches around my throat, and my eyes snap open, straight onto Bryant's. He takes my panties with his other hand and brings them to his nose, inhaling deeply. "Mine."

I look into his eyes, seeing his Dominant come out. "Yours."

He drops to his knees, and just like that, his mouth covers my clit and holy shit. I'm seeing stars. His tongue gliding over and between my folds as it hits my most sensitive of parts. Teasing, pleasuring, toying with every single aspect of myself. He knew exactly what to do and where to go as if he drew the damn map for my body. My breathing comes faster, as a groan erupts from my mouth. He stops. All pleasure I was just receiving stopping with his, and he gets to his feet. Stepping closer to me, he sucks my bottom lip into his mouth until every inch of my sweet tasting self owns my taste buds.

Wrapping his hands around the backs of my thighs, he picks me up and throws me down onto the kitchen bench, ripping his shirt off and then his pants. I inch up onto my elbows and watch as he massages his thick long cock with his hand as his eyes look over every inch of my exposed skin.

"You going to fuck me on the kitchen bench on our wedding night?"

He grins, getting up and crawling up my body. "Fucking right I am."

Beep
Beep
Beep

What's that sound?

I gasp loudly, my back arching off the bed as I get sucked out of my deep sleep, or memory, I've yet to figure out what is what. The dark night envelopes me in Bryant's—and I guess my—master bedroom, where he sleeps beside me.

I shiver, the cool wind of the night whisking through the open window and I throw my blanket off, walking around to close it. My silk robe now clings to my sweaty flesh as I push down on the window, closing out the busy night down below.

"Isa..." Bryant leans up on his elbows, watching me closely.

"Sorry, I didn't mean to wake you," I mutter, going back to bed and slipping back under the covers. "Just had a bad dream."

He pauses, I can see him watching me out of the corner of my eye. "You usually have dreams?"

I shrug. "Sometimes. Some are more vivid than others." I hit the lamp switch, cutting off the light again and sink into the bed, bringing the covers up to my mouth.

Silence.

Then suddenly, he gets up from bed and tugs on his sweatpants.

"What are you doing?"

Flicking on his side of the lamp, I turn over to see him throwing on a hoodie. "Going for a run."

I gaze at the time. "But it's four in the morning?"

"Your point?" he asks, annoyance etching into his features. I want to say that I thought he only ran at night but thought better of it. Even at this ungodly hour, fresh out of bed, he looks beautiful. It's not fair, he shouldn't be this good-looking.

"My point is it's four a.m.," I repeat, matching his annoyed tone.

He takes out some headphones and puts them into his ears before throwing his hoodie over his head. I open my mouth, about to say something else when he turns and leaves.

Huffing out, I lay back on my back and gaze up at the ceiling. Why doesn't he just kill me and get it over with?

Because dragging it out is worse, I guess. That must be what he's doing. This way, it lasts longer. Killing me would be too easy. But even as I think it, I know that there has to be more to this vendetta. Bryant Royal is calculated, smart, coherent. He's one hundred steps ahead of the human race and about three steps behind God. There's no outsmarting someone like him, there's not even a chance that I could work out what he's planning—but I'll try.

Tossing and turning, I settle for the fact that I won't be getting back to sleep anytime soon so I throw the covers off and get out of bed. Walking out of the master bedroom, I head down the stairs that lead to the main living areas when I hear the coffee pot starting up. Bryant must be home from his run. Wrapping my robe around my body, I enter the kitchen and stop dead in my tracks. It's not Bryant that's in there, it's another woman, dressed half naked, wearing nothing but lace panties and a man's white dress shirt.

Bryant's suit shirt—I'm guessing, since he's the only man that lives here.

"Ahh," I start, clearing my throat. If Bryant thinks he can fuck around on me under my own nose he has another thing coming. Even though I shouldn't care because our wedding is a fucking joke, still. It's the principle. "Who the fuck are you?" I quip, it's a step up from what Devon would have said—or done—thinking of Devon sets off a pang inside my chest. My yearning for him has intensified since last night, so I've decided I'm going to hunt him down today before calling my father to see if I can get any information out of him about this ridiculous fucking marriage.

Back to the slut in my kitchen.

The woman pauses, taking the mug from under the machine and bringing it to her lips, obviously unfazed by my intrusion.

She turns around slowly, smirking from beneath the rim. "I'm Jessica. And you are?" She tilts her head, looking me up and down. What the fuck is going on? And where the fuck is Bryant. And why is this bitch so damn fucking beautiful. Why the fuck am I even acknowledging that this bitch is beautiful? I need to get my cranium checked. We've been married for not even twenty-four hours, and he's already putting his dick into other girls. Hot girls. Fuck.

Fuck that.

"Isa..." I pause, then smirk. "Isa *Royal*."

Her mouth falls slightly before she places her mug on the kitchen table. "What the fuck has that idiot done."

"Pardon?" I quirk my eyebrow, confused about her stance or audacity.

She rolls her eyes, pulling a chair out from under the table and taking a seat. "I'm Jessica Royal. Bryant's sister."

The shock that falls over my face tells her enough. I didn't know Bryant had a sister, and nothing was said at the wedding either. Shit.

I tug out a chair and take a seat opposite her. She scans me, I scan her, both of us quite openly trying to assess each other. Then she hitches her thumb over her shoulder. "You don't want a coffee?"

I shake my head, the confusion still probably marred over my face. "No. Um, I don't mean to be rude, but I didn't know he had a sister?"

"Mmm." She places the mug onto the table, hiking a knee up. "He doesn't like to broadcast me that much because I'm a rebel that makes him look bad." She takes a sip of coffee. "And I also only just flew in from Paris this morning."

I laugh at her rebel comment, leaning back in my chair. We might get along. "I have to admit," I answer, flicking the rings around my fingers. "When I saw you standing here, I thought he had already put his dick where it shouldn't belong."

Jessica chokes on her coffee, banging her chest with her hand. "Shit," she laughs. "Sorry, it's just—and I mean this with no disrespect—but you're not really Bryant's type."

"So I figured," I answer, getting to my feet and deciding I need that coffee after all.

"I don't mean that as in a bad thing, I mean he usually sleeps with these suit looking girls who are shy and submissive. Not so... crass?" I pour coffee into a mug and go back to the table.

I know that Bryant hasn't been seen with another woman in the media, but I also know his appetite as a man. It's a very large appetite, and he's a very large man. The thought of tiny submissive girls being eaten by him flash through my brain and I chuckle.

"Well, I don't know how to answer that."

Her eyes narrow. "You look familiar; I'm trying to put my finger on it." Then she shakes her head, taking another sip of her coffee. "Must look like an actress or something."

I clear my throat. "Ahh, maybe, or might be because my father is Peter Johnson, as in the President."

Her eyes snap to mine, her dark long hair piling over her shoulders and her green eyes bright. "Oh my God!" She laughs, her straight white teeth showing through. She looks so much like Bryant. "Isa Johnson! I've heard of you and your party ways."

I lean back in my chair, blowing on my coffee. "Yeah, those were the good days."

"It makes sense now," she mutters.

"What does?" I tilt my head.

She pauses, looks at me and then takes a sip of coffee.

"My brother marrying you—no offense. But Bryant only ever does things if it works in his favor. He's a businessman first, and a brother/family man second. Business is always his number one."

I smile, nodding in agreement. "You have no idea." Bringing me back to my original question, I nudge my head toward her. "Do you live here?"

She shakes her head. "Nope, I just crash here whenever I'm in town, oh, and I ahhh... sleep with his security guard occasionally."

It's my turn to choke on my coffee now. "Shit. And he's okay with that?" I clear my throat.

She shrugs. "Definitely not, but he can't say anything."

I laugh. The thought of Bryant not being able to say anything is laughable. If there's any man walking this earth that will always be able to say something, it's Bryant. "Well, that's amusing," I whisper to myself, raking my long hair out of my face.

The front door opens and closes and my eyes shoot up toward it. Bryant walks in, his hoodie still over his head and his face drenched in sweat.

"That was a long run, brother dearest." Jessica bats her eyelashes at her brother, her head tilted backward.

"What the fuck are you doing here?" he growls, though I note, there was a softness to that growl.

"Ahh," she clicks her fingers, "the question is *who* am I doing here..."

"He's fired." Bryant yanks open the fridge and takes out a bottled water, twisting the cap off and taking a long drink while keeping his eyes locked on his baby sister.

"Bryant." Jessica gets off her chair and walks toward the sink. "Stop being ridiculous."

As if on cue, the bodyguard, one who I hadn't met yet,

(though that's not that unbelievable considering the time I've been in this world), walks into the kitchen, his shirt off and scratching his head. He's young, maybe mid-twenties.

Bryant turns to him. "You're fired. Pack your shit and be out before midday."

Then he turns to me. "What are you doing today?"

"Bryant! You're not being fair," Jessica moans like a sulking toddler.

Bryant looks at her over his shoulder. "You're right," then looks back to the bodyguard. "Pack your shit and be gone within the next half an hour."

Bringing his attention back to me, he raises his eyebrows. Guess that's my cue to answer, so I shrug, blowing into my mug of coffee until steam floats. "Find Devon, I suppose."

Bryant's face freezes. "Devon?"

I nod, looking at Jessica briefly, who is too busy eye-fucking her bodyguard to listen to our conversation. "Yes, my best friend and roommate who you sort of ripped me away from."

He shrugs as if it's no skin off his back, which it's not, but still, he could at least act like he feels a little like shit for ruining my life. Then he comes to me, leans down and places a kiss on my head. The gesture damn right threw me off because hell no is it like him at all. "We got a tone of shit to sort today." He inches back and looks into my eyes. "I'd appreciate If you were there."

A little taken back by his PDA, I whisper, "Sure," softly. He pushes off my chair and goes to walk out of the kitchen, glaring at Jessica. "Stop sleeping with my workers, Jess, or I will cut off your rights to come in and out." Then takes the stairs one at a time.

"Well, that was odd," Jessica looks like she's seen a ghost, her skin pale and her eyes as wide as saucers. I know she's not talking about his reaction to the bodyguard.

"Tell me about it," I mutter, standing up and emptying my cup in the sink.

The young bodyguard dude walks further into the kitchen. "Jessica, I can't lose my job."

"It'll be fine, you'll find another." She smiles, then winks at him. The girl is a savage. He shakes his head in disbelief but looks like he doesn't want to argue with her, and then walks out of the kitchen, back to wherever he came from. I really should ask Bryant about the arrangements around his house. I didn't even know that his workers stayed here.

She turns over her shoulder and looks at me. "We're going to be great friends." I'm sure we are, actually, I know we are. Tidying up the counter, I pack away the milk and other scatterings that are left out. I'm not tidy, not in the slightest. I drop my shit everywhere and I'm comfortable with that fact, but kitchen benches are one thing I can't stand to be messy. After I've cleaned, I make my way upstairs and into the master bedroom, taking in the beautiful view. The floor to ceiling windows mold the front of the room, casting a perfect view of the Upper East Side. The four post bed that sits opposite a large television and... oh my fucking God! I gasp, my hand coming to my mouth just as I hear Bryant walk into the room. "Is that?" I point to the artwork hanging on the wall, and no, it's not the Mona Lisa, but fuck me it may as well be. "Is that Mark Rothko's work?"

Bryant doesn't answer, so I turn to face him. He's smirking. Of course he is. Smug asshole. I change tactics because it obviously is Rothko's work, and forgive me art gods, I'm only saying this to wipe the smug look off of Bryant's face.

Shrugging, I grin. "Figures you'd own Mark Rothko."

That gets his attention because he cocks his head and

pushes off the wall, coming into the room more. "And why do you say that?"

"Well, isn't it obvious?" I look directly at him now, my eyes dancing with mischief. "The artwork is about as bland as you." Now, I only know his work because Lydia has one of his pieces in her library, and I don't know, I've always been fascinated by art and people's different views of one picture.

After a long pause, Bryant throws his head back and laughs. "Oh, ok, and who would you have hanging on your wall, hmmm?"

I don't even have to think. It's instant. "Alec Monopoly or Banksy."

"Jesus fucking Christ," Bryant groans, shaking his head. "Isa, that isn't..."

"Don't say it, Royal. Don't say it."

"Fine." He rolls his eyes. "But there will be none of that on my walls."

Yeah, we'll see. He turns his head toward the shower. "Won't be long."

I cast a look to the bathroom, sucking my bottom lip in and nod. "Sure." Before I can think about getting in with him, the bathroom door closes. I quite like this side of Bryant. The carefree side, I hope I see more of that side through this completely false marriage. Walking into the closet, I take out some skinny jeans and a casual tank top. I hope wherever he's taking me doesn't have a dress code because even if it did, I wouldn't change. Yes, it's so official, Bryant and I are complete worlds apart.

After I've changed, I pull a brush through my long hair just as a voice clears from behind me. I whip my head toward the bathroom door to find Bryant standing there naked with nothing but a towel wrapped around his waist. The water cascades down his six-pack abs and then disappears somewhere between the edges of his V. So me not going in there was obviously a shit decision because now my lady parts are fucking tingling like no one's business. Well, Bryant's business, but you catch my drift. That body is really not fair, and what's even worse, I know what it feels like under my fingertips. What it tastes like on the tip of my tongue, and how his thigh muscles clench when—"Isa?" Bryant interrupts my dirty thoughts, and I quickly look up to meet his eyes, my cheeks flashing hot. Fuck.

"Yes?" I answer innocently, eyebrows quirked, a shit attempt at coming off as casual, though I'm guessing I'm making it more obvious the more I try to hide it, so I tilt my head and look over his arms.

"Wanna take a picture, babe? It'll last longer."

"Don't flatter yourself, I just have a healthy sexual appetite and I must say..." I tease, slowly making my way toward the bed. New strategy: distraction. "It's been a while since I've been fed." You know, distract him away from the fact that I just got caught checking him out, but the way his eyes haven't moved from mine and the way his shoulders are jiggling from laughter, I'd say I'm not winning. I'm beginning to realize I very rarely win when it comes to him, too.

"Get changed." He nudges his head toward the closet, breaking through that fucking laugh.

"Why? Where we going?" I brush off, trying not to sound offended by his blatant rejection.

He walks into the closet. "Stop asking questions."

11

I should have asked more questions. Stepping out of the car, I close the passenger door. "Where are we?" We drove around for an hour out of the city, and again, I definitely should have asked more questions because this building is... strange. The structure had to be built in the early twenties—maybe before then. The old brick looks to be held together by green moss, and the old Victorian windows are framed by white wood. It's elegant, yet a little disturbing.

Bryant shuts off his Audi Q7 right outside the large concrete steps that lead up to equally wide twin doors. There's a little doorknocker that hangs off it, carved as a lion's head. Ha. Perfect. Fits the creepy house to a T.

"So where'd you bring me? Don't tell me you married me, let me off on your brother's..." I look around, uncomfortable with talking about it so openly. "*You know*... all for you to bring me here and kill me..."

He quirks an eyebrow and grins cockily, putting a cigarette between his teeth. He sparks it, and then blows the smoke out slowly, walking around the car toward me. "You know damn well you are too expensive to kill." He winks at me and then nudges his head. "Ready to have lunch with the olds?"

Oh Lord.

Okay, now I wish it was a torture house. Now, I know I said how lovely his parents are, but I would still prefer a little warning. The prick obviously knew that.

"Uhhh..." I answer absently, and when he leaves me in the dust by heading to the front door, I quickly catch up to him. Since the wedding day, I've noticed a slight change in Bryant. He's not being as cold as usual, and I don't know if that's all part of his plan, but I'm not going to complain. If only he could break and give me more sex. I mean, we had sex last night—yes, but I'm a girl with needs, very demanding needs, and I'm seriously in need right now. His hands running down my navel—

"Isa!" he snaps at me from the top of the stairs.

"Coming." I walk up toward him, clearing my throat from my quite obvious daydream.

He grins down at me, right when the front doors swing open. "What were you thinking about just now?"

I look up into his eyes, searching their dark green depths. "I—"

"Son!" his mom greets with open arms. Because the wedding went so fast, I don't remember either of his parent's names and I feel terrible for it. I'm hoping Bryant introduces us again or, I get a random outburst of remembering.

"Mother." Bryant hugs his mom, and I see the side of his eyes soften at her embrace. Looking back toward his father, I see him smile at me, but it doesn't have quite the same warm effect as when Bryant's mother smiles at me.

"Isa." He gives me a curt nod, rather formally.

I reply with a soft smile. "Hello."

"Isa, oh I'm so excited. I found a whole bunch of old baby photos as I was clearing out some old things in the attic," Bryant's mom announces as she ushers me into the house.

My eyes go wide as I peek a look over my shoulder at Bryant, unable to stop his persistent mother from dragging me into the house. His mom is not what you'd expect from a rich family. Not saying that most rich families are snobby, but her son is, and eighty percent of the wealthy population tend to have gold cactus launched up their asses. It's why I love Devon and my little life in New Orleans so much.

I chuckle under my breath with found realization at how uncomfortable Bryant must be what with his mom showing me his baby photos and all.

She gestures into the vast living room where couches are sprawled out tidily. It's cozy, warm, and inviting—not so much how I interpreted it from the outside. "Have a seat, Isa. I'm so sorry that we didn't get much time to chat after the wedding." She takes a seat on the sofa opposite me and crosses her legs at her ankles. Despite the fact that I was raised in a wealthy home and my father is who he is, good, or even decent, etiquette has never been my strong suit. Or any suit. In fact, I don't wear suits, I wear ripped jeans and tanks, and by my memory, my legs are open more than they're crossed. Especially by my ankles.

"Oh truly, it's no problem." I add a hint of a sweet smile with my reply, like I wasn't just thinking about my legs being open. "Everything has moved rather fast, wedding day included."

"That is true, I guess," she confirms, as a maid walks into the room carrying a silver platter and placing it on the little coffee table that sits between us.

Bryant's mom smiles at me briefly with a small flick of

her eyelashes. Leaning over to pour tea into both china mugs, she sneaks a glance at me. "Autumn," she answers my unspoken question innocently.

"Pardon?" I question, taking the mug she's handing me. I place it on my lap as she sits back in the sofa.

"My name." She quirks an eyebrow, but it's not in a snobby judgmental way, more in a way as she knew I didn't know her name but she was saving me the embarrassment of having to ask.

"Shit." I let out a defeated sigh, my shoulders slacking. "I'm so sorry." I truly do feel terrible. I mean, Jesus, I don't even know my mother-in-law's name.

She giggles, taking a sip of her tea and leans back into her chair. "It's entirely not your fault. If my son had done this the traditional way, we wouldn't have had this issue." I hear the word 'son' in slow motion and watch as her mouth curves around each syllable. It sets something off inside of me. Up until this point, I had forgotten all about Bryant's brother and what I had done. It's made me somewhat realize how dangerously close I have been riding to the 'attachment' line. I can't let this feeling get too comfortable, with her, or anyone in his family, or hell, even Bryant, because truthfully, I still don't know what it is he actually wants with me (if my gut is correct which tells me it's not just because of my father, but again, my gut has been wrong in the past), and also, if I do manage to build a solid foundation with his family, what will happen when they find out what I'd done? I'd lose more people, so no, I need to remember what is going on right now and not get sucked into Bryant's... whatever the fuck kind of juju he manages to put over me.

"So! Photos!" Autumn grins, pulling a large —and what looks to be very heavy—chest over toward her. I go to get up off my chair, wanting to help her because honestly, it looks heavier than her, when I hear Bryant's voice from behind me. "Mom..." he warns, and I cast a glance over my shoulder. Walking in with an unlit cigar between his fingers comes the king himself.

"Oh, Bryant. Leave us alone to talk gossip, and go back to your father."

Bryant looks at me and then looks back to his mom. Can he read my mind? Can he see that I had a brief moment of sadness, thinking about his brother? How will I react when I see a photo of his brother? Will it set off a panic attack followed by a shit storm of drama as I unintentionally display my guilty memories for everyone to see?

"Come..." Bryant nudges his head toward the double porch doors, breaking through my slight panic. Everything sucks back into reality, and I look back at Autumn, not really wanting to leave her because I don't want to come off as rude, but also, I sort of want to leave just in case that scenario I played out in vivid detail inside my head becomes a reality.

Yikes.

We can't have that.

I plaster one of my go-to cute smiles at her, hoping she will maybe let me off the hook.

She rolls her eyes with (what I think is) a knowing smile. "Newlyweds. Don't be too long. I have some good photos here."

I stand to my feet. "Thank you for the tea, Autumn, I won't be long."

She smiles sweetly and then flips open an album, getting lost back in what I'm guessing is some of her most favorable memories. I've not thought about having children much, only because, well, I don't know, I haven't thought about it. Between cankles, the feeling of your guts and ovaries being ripped open and then your vajayjay *literally* getting ripped open, it lost its appeal. Not to mention mom friends.... Yeah, I don't see how that would go down very well considering my favorite F word is 'fuck' and my second favorite F word is Friday because Friday usually means drinking followed by getting fucked.

Point being, I'd be a shit mom, so I'm doing the universe a favor, it would seem.

Bryant tugging on my arm brings me out of my reverie, so I follow him out the porch doors, the late afternoon sun kissing my skin instantly and the whispering sound of wind whirling between the branches of the trees.

"Why'd you save me from that back there?" I ask as we step onto the damp grass. The entire outdoors in the back is set like some old English manor. Thick large shrubs line the vast paddock, and a large round fountain sits right in the middle.

Bryant shrugs. "Only seems fair, and I don't really want Mom and Dad to know that my new wife was the person who murdered their son."

I snap my mouth closed, just as a boulder-size ball of nerves sets at the core of my throat. "That's not fair."

He stops and then stares at me. His eyes scream authority. "A lot of shit isn't fair, Isa, with the amount of time you use that line, it's starting to lose its effect, but for argument's sake, how so?"

I flinch, looking away from him. He's right about the whole a lot of shit isn't fair thing, and I wish I could give him a valid answer. "I don't know, but I was sort of hoping that with us now married, the brother jabs would lessen." There, that wasn't so bad.

He disregards me with a lazy lip curl before continuing to walk toward the backyard.

"Can I ask you something?" I catch up to him before walking at his casual pace beside him.

"No."

Nice try.

"Well, I'm going to ask you anyway..."

"Figured," he mutters. He slows his walking pace, shoving his hands into his pockets.

"Were you close to your brother?" He doesn't flinch with my question, but he doesn't answer either. We remain in silence until I see we've walked the entire space of the yard and now we're right at where a pool house is built, tucked away discretely. It's a little more modern than the main house which means it must be newer, and by the judge of the structure, a lot newer. It's all glass walls, black marble, and more glass. Whereas the main house, well, I thought it was a sex torture chamber, so that says enough.

Bryant starts, heading toward the glass sliding doors and opening them. "No, we weren't." I exhale out a breath of air, all though I don't know why I'm relieved from this revelation. Close or not, it was still his brother. I guess a small part of me was hoping... birds of a feather and all that shit...that he wasn't like him.

I follow him into the pool house.

He must read my sudden relaxed expression because he scoffs, legit scoffs, while closing the door. "Just because I wasn't close with him, does not mean I'm not a bad man, Isa. We were two different kinds of bad."

If I weren't so stubborn, I'd cringe right here because damnit it all, he can read my damn mind. "What kind of bad are you?" I ask teasingly, making sure my shoulder brushes against his hard chest as I prance past him.

I feel his chin brush over my shoulder as his breath touches the nape of my neck. He leans into my ear. "The kind you can't kill." Then bites down on my shoulder roughly.

Yelp! This man is on a whole other level, but I smirk. "I could have fun trying," I answer, looking at him over my shoulder. He narrows his eyes at me and for a few seconds, we stare at each other for a beat too long. My stomach clenches and my nipples harden and suddenly, I feel like the submissive girl he loves to play with all over again, but this, this is pushing the rules. I'm only submissive in bed—there's no way I'd let him tell me what to do outside of the bedroom or where there's no sexual shenanigans going on. Maybe I need to start some shenanigans. Breaking our eye contact, I look forward and see a lap pool and watch as the water glistens from the late afternoon sun setting on it. Glancing up, I see that the entire roof is clear glass, which gives you a direct view of the sky. I think it's my favorite place of the house. I respect the character of the main house, but for some reason, out here feels a little less haunted. Around the pool, there are lounge chairs and canopies and directly in front of us, there's a rectangular bar that overlooks everything.

"It's beautiful out here." I take in the glass walls, the glass ceiling and glass bar. "Seriously, really beautiful."

"Yeah," Bryant agrees, stepping forward so that he's beside me. "They wanted it after my brother went missing..."

I pause. "Missing?" I look at him.

He glances down at me. "Yes, missing. They don't know that he's dead. They think he's missing." He continues further into the pool house, heading straight to the bar.

I follow. "Huh. I guess I never asked how you managed to... you know, the body and stuff after..."

"And you won't."

"I won't?" I question, pulling up a bar stool and taking a seat.

"No." He uses his firm voice. Which I'm starting to think that he uses it a lot with me. "You won't. The less you know about what happened *after*, the better." He takes down a bottle of whiskey and grabs two glasses before walking back around and taking a seat beside me. He grips onto my chair, spinning me around to face him then proceeds to pour whiskey into each glass.

"We're going to play a game."

Oh Lord.

"Hmmm," I tease, taking the glass he's handing me. "What kind?"

He loses his tie and pops the first few buttons off of his collar, displaying the tip of what I know is a very ripped and very tanned chest. My mouth waters. I throw my leg over the other one to cross my legs in an attempt to calm the throbbing ache that has started in between my legs—

He laughs, tossing back his whiskey.

"Something funny?" I quirk an eyebrow and take a small sip of my drink. There's no way I'm losing control with alcohol, who knows what I'd say. I'm not worried what I'd do, just my mouth. It always seems to get me in trouble.

"Yeah, the fact that you're insatiable *is* rather funny."

"I'm in control. Complete control." I stretch my arms wide to accentuate my point. My point is pretty bent because I'm not in control at all. He makes me all… stupid.

He regards me by pouring more whiskey. "We're playing twenty-one questions." I can do this. I think. I can lie, I'm rather good at lying. I look at Bryant, his eyes connecting with mine and holding my attention far too effortlessly for my comfort.

Ok, nope. I don't think I can lie to that. Fuck.

I throw back another shot of whiskey. "Is this like husband-wife bonding time?"

His eyes narrow at me in obvious annoyance. "Something like that."

"Okay, fine, I'll start!" Down goes another shot, to hell with not losing control, this is going to be torturous. "Do I annoy you?"

"Oh that's easy." He grins, and goddamn I would give my left arm to see that grin again. Not really, because I'm left-handed so that arm is pretty important, but Bryant always has a great grin. "Yes. Daily." He finishes with a wink. "My turn..." I'm not even surprised by that answer, I wanted to start easy. You don't fuck someone in the ass on the first date.

Or do you.

He runs his tongue over his bottom lip. Shit. That was hot too. Focus. I need to focus. "How many times have you orgasmed in one session?"

Well, it appears, Bryant does fuck someone in the ass on the first date. He hits it raw too, no lube.

I choke on my whiskey.

"Oh shit." He pats my shoulder sarcastically. "It seems you had a different idea about twenty-one questions." Then he laughs and relaxes back into his chair.

I narrow my eyes at him, swiping my mouth with the back of my hand. "I don't know. There was this one time... I think, it's like four."

"Four."

I nod. "Four." Holding four fingers up before grabbing the bottle and pouring more into my cup. "My turn!" I place the bottle back onto the counter. "Do you hate me?"

He's still silent by my number revelation, but he searches

my eyes and seems to think over my question. "What? Like in the bedroom or everyday living?"

I shrug. "I don't know, either..."

He seems to mull over my question. A couple jaw clenches later, he answers, "Yes." I down my entire drink. Okay, so his hate is real.

"Why did you have sex with Devon?" He flicks his glass away from him slightly.

"Because it's comfortable..." I begin while thinking what I should say next and of course, taking control of the bottle of whiskey. "He knows what I like and how I like it. He needs it as bad as I do and it just, I don't know. It always worked for us."

Bryant nods. "I get that." He does?

Wow. I'm shocked.

Knowing it's my turn, I look right into his eyes. "Why do you keep asking me about sex? Why no real questions?"

He chuckles, his cold eyes flicking blankly over my shoulder. "Because I know everything else that there is to know about you, Isa."

"You're cocky."

"Very. And I have a big one, so..."

"You're not very funny though..." I lie, the effects of the alcohol slowly slipping into the driver's seat of my thoughts.

"I don't want to be funny."

"I like funny."

"And I don't give a fuck what you like."

My eyes narrow. His narrow back.

"I don't believe you."

"What?" He chuckles. "That I don't know everything that there is to know about you?"

Long pause. "Yes. I don't believe you."

His glass dangles lazily between his fingers as he tilts his head and runs his piercing eyes up and down my body. Slowly but surely, it's as if he's undressing me with his stare. "Isa Maree Johnson, one sister, mom ran away when you were a baby, sister is the poster child of the family, you're the rebel—one of the reasons why your favorite color is black— you have three piercings, three tattoos, childhood best friend—except for Devon—was Jennifer Black, first car was a piece of shit Honda, you play the lottery for the excitement even though you know you'd never win and you have enough money in your trust account to put the lottery winners to shame, oh, and you've always wanted to be an architect." My mouth is still open when he finishes because everything he said was spot-on. I'm appalled. And a little turned on.

"How?"

He grabs his drink again. "I knew everything about you before you even knew I existed."

Standing from his chair, he looks down at me and I look up at him, my eyes crossing slightly at the angle. Pulling my bottom lip into my mouth, I run my eyes down his long massive body and then stop near his zipper.

I need to touch him.

Reaching up, I press the palm of my hand against his chest, and his eyes close in response. Standing to my feet slowly, I unbutton his dress shirt with one pop at a time. Just as I hit the final button, his eyes slam open, straight onto mine, with fire burning deep inside of them. He drops his forehead down to my own before kissing me, his soft lips pressing against mine. He's a great kisser. Usually, he's raw, rough, and there's always a lot of tongue but this one is tender. Still a lot of tongue and still rough, but the pace of his tongue massaging mine is slower. I lose control slightly, moaning into his mouth while wrapping my arms around his neck. He palms my ass, gripping my cheek tightly while grinding me into his massive bulge. I grind against it until a low groan escapes him and he's picking me up off the ground. My legs wind around his waist all while we never break out of our intimate kiss. Then the kissing turns frantic, desperate. He steps forward until my back collides against the wall, my head hitting the glass with a thud. Gripping my breast from under my dress, he tears my dress off of my body and throws it to the ground before ripping my bra off and sucking a nipple into his mouth.

"For the record, I didn't plan this..." he smirks, hooking his finger into my panties and yup you guessed it, tearing the suckers right off.

Stepping backward, while taking all of my nakedness in, he smirks. Now, I don't know the full details of why he married me, I mean, I know it has to do with my dad and making my life miserable, but right now, he's not succeeding with the miserable side—in fact, I'm getting rather annoyed at how something nudges in my chest every time he looks at me with his hungry predatory glare.

"Fuck me," I blurt out before I dive headfirst into feelings I don't particularly want to so much as test the waters with right now.

He drops to his knees, tossing my leg over his shoulder and blows on my clit until my back is arching off the wall and my wetness dripping down my inner thigh. "After I've eaten."

COMING DOWN SLIGHTLY with sweat dripping off my skin, I feel my eyes getting drowsy and heavy. Leaning against the glass wall while clutching his suit jacket around my naked body, I watch as he gets up from the floor butt naked and saunters toward the bar, taking out a couple of bottled waters from the fridge. I take that time to tilt my head and watch his perfect ass flex with each step. Then he's frontal, his gigantic heavy dick right there as he comes back to me with a smug grin on his face, tossing a bottle at me. His usually perfectly styled hair is sitting all messy and unruly on the top of his head and his abs are glistening against the dim bar light. The sun has far since set and now the sky is filled with bright stars that are twinkling over us.

Bryant leans against the wall beside me, taking a gulp of water.

I laugh. "So much for twenty-one questions."

He swallows. "Well, we got to four."

"True..." I shake my head. "I don't think I've ever had sex with someone who hates me, though." There's a long pause. I didn't mean it to sound like I was sad about it, or that I even cared, but the fact that my stupid fucking filter didn't do me a solid when it should have and now Bryant is going to think that out of those four questions, that was the one that got to me, yeah, that fact annoys me.

"There's a first time for everything." Then he pauses. Well, he's always honest, I have to give him that. "I don't want to hate you, Isa." He pushes off the wall and stands directly in front of me with each hand on either side of my head, caging me in. He's so close that I can feel his bulge pressing against my belly. He looks between each of my eyes, his eyebrows pulled in slightly. "Hate is an easy feeling for me to embrace. I feed off of it. Better I feel *something*, even if it is hate."

"I get it." I shake my head, hanging my head slightly. The first time since this whole thing started, I feel a tone of different emotions running wild inside of me. "I deserve it too, I guess."

"No, you don't."

My eyes snap back up to his, shocked by his answer. "I don't?"

"No, Isa..." he glares back at me. It's a stare that says don't fucking question my sincerity of my answer. I let him carry on because of this. "I used it as a nesting ground to force you to marry me so I could destroy your life. To make me feel better, but truth is, Justin had it coming. He was a convicted sex offender. My parents? They paid it all away constantly. He was eventually going to pay for his wrongs. I'm only sorry it had to be you that had to live with it, 'cuz I sure as fuck know I almost killed him—more than once."

"I'm sorry," is all I can muster to say.

"Sorry for what?" He pushes off the wall and I feel as though a huge weight had been taken away with him.

"You lost your brother."

Bryant shrugs casually. "As I said, he had it coming."

Not wanting to let this one thing go, I ask, "Why did you marry me, Bryant."

He chuckles, tugging his clothes back on. "I'll tell you one day."

"When?"

"When I don't hate you anymore, and when I trust you." Then he points to his jacket. "You might need to leave that on... since your dress is ruined."

Shit.

"Bryant!" I half laugh and half annoyed snap at him, shaking my head. "Your parents are going to see us in this state."

He shrugs. "Jess has some clothes here you can wear if it bothers you that much. We'll eat dinner and leave."

. . .

WE ATE DINNER, and I slipped into some of Jess's clothes, even though she's a whole dress size smaller than me. Dinner talk was easy, carefree. Around all the laughs about Bryant's childhood photos, and the sangria, it was a breeze and I felt as though I had known, particularly his mother, longer than what I actually had.

12

BRYANT

Isa hugs my mom and dad goodbye before we get into my car. Seeing her little body against my dad's almost makes me laugh because he's built like a caveman and she's so tiny. I could snap her with a simple flick of my wrist. I want to snap her. I want to snap her bad. Truth is, I can't let go of this feeling of wanting to hurt her. She reminds of that day every time I see her. It's not really that day though, I couldn't give a fuck about Justin, and that's the God honest truth. The fucker had it coming, and if Isa didn't do it, I would have eventually. The little fuck was always spoilt and always had Mom and Dad bailing him out of every single shit mess he had created. Since he has been gone, my mother hasn't touched a drink and my father has been around the house more often. It's as if his "disappearance" is unspoken, but it was healthy for our family. He put a lot of bullshit on all of our plates. Jessica was the one I knew would be okay with it the most. Well, as okay as you can be. Justin spent most of his time and life tormenting her when-ever I wasn't around. He'd lock her in the attic for days on end while Dad was out on business and Mom was too drunk to register. She was his very own doll that he would use as he pleased. When the first round of sexual abuse case came around, we had to sit down and ask Jessica if there was anything that we needed to know. Just to be sure, and because with Justin, you'd never know.

"Are you crazy? No. He would hit me and get great pleasure on inflicting pain on me but no, he never sexually touched me." Which was a fucking good thing, because I would have ended him that day—no questions asked, if he had. Other than that, we don't talk about it. It never did make much sense to me though because he didn't actually need to rape women. He was good-looking, he could've probably had anyone he wanted, but he needed to force himself onto them. It was what got him off. He said he had gotten better as years went on, but he hadn't.

"Damn." Isa breaks through my thoughts, tidying her hair as I drive out onto the busy road. "I feel like a whore."

"Whore's get paid. You rode my dick for free." I see her head snap toward me out of the corner of my eye, so I smirk.

Gotta admit, seeing her in my jacket earlier with her hair all up in a messy ponytail almost had me punching in my man card and dropping to her knees. Fuck. Even thinking something like that has me worried as shit. This wasn't part of the plan. I wasn't supposed to get attached to her—and I'm not attached to her— but I do find myself slowly warming up to her annoying tendencies and finding them, at times, the times when I don't want to strangle her, a little cute.

Cute? The fuck.

I need to go by the office to get her the fuck out of my head. Maybe drown myself in some worthless pussy to remind myself that Isa Johnson—fuck—Isa Royal, does not mean shit to me. But the thought of having any other girl but Isa wrapped around my dick has him doing a duck and hide. Fuck.

"Bryant?" She waits for me to answer whatever she just said, but I don't know what the fuck she asked because I was too busy thinking about bending her over the bar and smashing her cervix open as I yanked on that sexy little ponytail—*fuck*.

"Yeah?" Fuck it, I'll wing it and act like I heard whatever the fuck she was yapping about.

"Can we stop at iHop? I feel like pancakes."

I smirk. Pancakes. My girl likes pancakes. I'll be damned. "Done."

I called her my girl.

I need a new swear word because 'fuck' is losing its effect.

Fuck.

"Bryant? Your three o'clock is here..." Dahlia, my assistant, knocks on my door. Which is a good thing, considering all I can think about is our pancake trip last night. Isa went on about her family and how distant they all are. She didn't need to tell me, though, I pegged that the first time I ever met her father, Mr. President. He's not a good sort, not even in the slightest, but I voted for him. Why? Because he gives a shit about America, and anyone who gives a shit about 'Merica, I have time for. Not like the rest of the pussy-footers who had previously run our government. We needed a soldier, a mother-fucking marine, and he is all those things. His fatherly love wasn't a part of my voting equation and I will probably vote him again. Her stepmom, Lydia, sounds nuts, but the way Isa's tone changes when she talks about her tells me that there is a slight air of compassion toward her. More than what she shows her father. Her sister sounds nuts too. In fact, they all do. Which is ironic because Isa says she's the outcast of the family, but the more I get to know her, she's not the outcast—it's her family who are the outcasts.

"Yeah, bring him in." I don't remember who the fuck my three o'clock is, and I'm pretty sure I didn't actually book someone for three, but I haven't been on top of my game much lately, and it has everything to do with a green-eyed brunette who currently bears my last name.

Fucking Isa.

"Royal!" I bring my eyes up to the door and see Devon, Isa's best-friend walk through the door. I lean back in my chair lazily, an eyebrow raised.

"Devon." I give him one of my grins as he takes a seat. "I don't remember having a three o'clock appointment."

"Funny." He leans back in his chair, his jaw clenching. "I don't remember having to book an appointment."

"What can I do for you?" I glare at him, trying to hide the smug look on my face. Smug because I know how much he must hate that Isa, the girl he's been in love with for years, is bouncing on my dick now. I discretely readjust myself, squashing any thoughts of Isa 'bouncin' on my dick.'

Fuck.

"You can tell me why my cousin decided to marry my best friend."

I can't even stop the laugh that escapes me. "Ahh, knew that would be what you wanted."

Devon leans on his elbow. "I'm serious, B. Why the fuck did you marry Isa. Has this got to do with me? You hate me that much, huh?"

I take back my earlier statement about Isa's family being all fucked up. I can't judge, my family would give them a run for their money. And we both have a lot of fucking money.

"Why would this have anything to do with you?" I ask, slightly insulted that he would think I gave a fuck about his existence enough to marry someone just for his discomfort.

He continues to glare at me from across the room. "Why, then?"

I lean forward, tapping on my computer keyboard. "A few reasons, none of which are any of your business. And by the way, why have you stopped talking to her? You didn't even make the wedding." I grin, putting a cigarette between my teeth and sparking it up with my Zippo. "I'm rather insulted."

"You don't get insulted," he answers deadpan. He's right, I don't, and I might be fishing for a reason to knock his teeth out just for shits and giggles because it's been a long time since I've knocked someone the fuck out.

He gets up from his chair, throwing his hoodie over his head. "Bryant, you hurt her and I will kill you."

Now, this would be the perfect time, but I'm too zen to give a fuck, so I smirk. "Noted."

He leaves like a sore loser who didn't get the last cookie in the jar. And he didn't. He didn't get any cookies in the jar because I don't just own the cookies now, I own the jar and the whole damn kitchen. Typical Devon, needs reminding where his place is when he tries to come against me, which is about one hundred steps below.

The convenience of Devon being her roommate was too coincidental, but I didn't plan it that way at all, and I wasn't lying when I said that it had nothing to do with him. Because it has everything to do with her father. All I have to do now is make sure I don't let that fucking smile or stupid fucking laugh get under my skin.

I WATCH *as Isa bolted out the tent, shocked and distraught—and as she should. She just killed someone after all... my brother. This wasn't part of the plan and Justin was supposed to keep himself under control. This time he chose wrong though because Isa was obviously a take no shit kinda girl. Good to know.*

"Bryant, man, what are we going to do about this mess?" Isaac stressed, his face pale and his lips blue. It's almost as if he was the one who killed him. Little bitch. I didn't blame him though, the sight wasn't an easy one to swallow.

"I have someone." I tilted my head.

"You have someone?" Bobby scoffed, taking a seat on the bed in the far corner of the tent. His head drops to the palm of his hands while he started to rock gently. He was about to lose it, no doubt, but that was Bobby. Always was the one to flip out over the smallest of things, so yeah, this sight probably kicked up his 'lose it' meter a lot.

"Yes," I hissed, looking at him. "Of course I fucking do."

"How can you be so easy about this? This is your brother! I mean, I know that you both haven't been very close since—ever but still..." Bobby continued, looking at the motionless body on the floor.

"Because I hated him." I pulled out my phone and pressed call on The Reaper. He answered on the second ring.

"Royal. Well, I wish I could say that I was surprised, but I'm not."

I blurted out the location of where we were and hung up my phone, looking back to Isaac. "He's on his way. Once he's done his job, and he's very good at his job, I'll get the crew to pack away this tent."

"But you didn't get the girl..." Isaac whispered, looking at me.

"No, I didn't, but I will. She's mine. She just doesn't know it yet."

13

ISA

My phone vibrating on my bedside table brings me out of my painting trance. I set up my easel right beside the glass window that overlooks downtown New York. I spent all day shopping for supplies because I couldn't get my paint shipped from New Orleans and it be here on time. Tilting my head at the murky black shadows that I have painted on the canvas, I wipe my hands on a rag while answering my phone.

"Hello?" I'm still trying to figure out my new painting. It's all dark shadows and blood when Devon's voice shocks me out of my daze.

"Isa..."

"Devon!" I screech, looking down at my phone to see an unknown number displayed.

"Yeah, I'm sorry, boo. Can you talk?"

"I'm mad at you." I place my brush back on the stand and walk to the large window.

"I know."

"Really mad."

He sighs. "I know."

"Want to do lunch?" I ask, already slightly over my being mad at him.

"Sure. Donut King?"

I smile, my stomach rumbling at the thought of deep-fried goodness. "See you there soon." Hanging up my phone, I have a quick shower and toss some jeans and a T-shirt on before slipping out of the penthouse and onto the busy street of downtown, of course, with Jerry and a couple MIB's following very closely.

"Mrs. Royal," Brian, Bryant's driver gestures toward the black SUV. Brian and Bryant. Cute. Sounds like the beginning of a true bromance story. "I can take you where you need to go."

I bite down my quirky thoughts. "Of course. Thank you." Brian, who must be in his late fifties, opens the back door of the Range Rover, gesturing for me to get in.

I look back to Jerry and he nods, getting one of his men to get their car.

The drive to Donut King wasn't long, like I had expected. I knew it wasn't very far from where we were. He pulls up to the curb and gets out, opening my door.

I nod at him politely. "Thanks, Brian. I can text you when I need you to collect me."

Brian cranks his neck until it clicks. "It's no problem, Mrs. Royal. I can wait for you here."

I still don't know if or when I will ever get used to being 'Mrs. Royal.'

I pause, watching him closely. "Bryant put you up to this, didn't he?"

Brian gives me an apologetic smile. At least he looks a little bit sorry, even if he's not. "Yes, ma'am."

"You can call me Isa, Brian." He shuffles slightly. "Unless it makes you more comfortable calling me Mrs. Royal?"

He nods. "I'm afraid I feel more comfortable referring to you as that."

Patting his arm, his big, strong arm, I reply, "Okay, and I will try not to be long."

He shakes his head. "Take as long as you need." Then I turn around and walk into the large purple store. The smell hits me instantly, deep-fried pastries sprinkled in warm cinnamon and brown sugar then dipped in chocolate syrup, maybe. Oh, or caramel syrup. My stomach grumbles loudly, making it known just how hungry I am. Damn, I feel as though I've died and gone to heaven. I see Devon's back facing me and my heart rate picks up again. Coming up behind him, I quickly wrap my arms around his neck from behind and he instantly jolts up from his chair in surprise, picks me up, and spins me around.

"Hey, trouble…" he whispers into the crook of my neck.

I relax, all my nerves contracting as I let out a long sigh. "Hey, mischief."

He puts me back down to my feet, pushing me back softly before gazing at me up and down. "Marriage looks good on you, señorita."

I roll my eyes and take a seat on the chair opposite him. Devon has always been a terrible liar. "Stop bullshitting."

"No lies." He shakes his head, and it's then that I notice how the skin around his eyes are wrinkled at the edges and his jaw has a few days scruff on it. Not like Devon at all, he's always been a strong advocate for the 'no beard' campaign. I don't know if there is such a campaign because you wouldn't catch me dead in it, but Devon would definitely be the ringleader of the entire operation, equipped with a big flag that would read 'No Beards' across it. Riding horses are cool, but have you ever ridden a beard? I have, and let me tell you...

Yikes. I'm getting distracted.

"You look good." I remove my jacket and toss it over the chair beside me.

"Now who's lying." He gestures to the waiter and then looks back to me. "I'm sorry, Isa."

"No." I shake my head. "I don't care anymore." I place my hand over his. "All that matters is that I have you back."

His eyes remain on mine, his jaw clenching a few beats and then he abruptly yanks his hand away, his eyes finding the waiter's. "Can I get two caramel filled donuts, one long black, and one latte." The waiter scribbles his order down and then walks off.

"Devon?" I raise my eyebrows, trying to gain his attention. "I do have you back—right?"

He stares down at his glass of water and then picks it up. "Honestly, Isa, I don't know." He leans forward as he reaches for my hand but it's my turn to yank it away from him. Tugging on his hair in obvious frustration, he leans back on his chair again. "What we've been, *how* we've known each other...I just—I don't think it's going to be as easy to change from that to something more mainstream."

Mainstream. If there was anything to sum up Devon and I's friendship, it would not be mainstream.

I gaze out the window. "Why is that hard, Devon?" I look back at him. "It's simple. We are still friends, we just don't do that side of what we used to do."

He laughs, but it's a bitter laugh, not a light laugh. Not a laugh I've heard come from Devon. "Oh, right, and so I should just forget how you use to come to me when you needed sex or anything? Or I should forget how your skin felt under the palm of my hand?" He tilts his head. "How am

I supposed to forget all those things, Isa? How am I supposed to forget the moans that would leak out of you right before you'd combust all over my dick."

"Devon!" I look around the restaurant, hoping no one heard his little outburst. Regardless whether or not that he would find it hard, I thought we had always been clear about where we stood with each other. It was always just sex and that's why when we would have sex with other people, it was never a big deal. "Devon..." I change my tone to a whisper. "Do you have feelings for me?"

The waiter comes over placing the donuts and the two coffees down. "Here you go..." he smiles, but both Devon and I are glaring at each other from across the table, none of us flinching, and he doesn't have to say it because I see it there. Point blank right in his face that he does, in fact, have feelings for me. The waiter leaves once the silence gets uncomfortable.

"How long?" I ask, picking up my coffee.

"Too long," he mutters, taking a drink of his coffee after blowing on it.

"Devon, you can't—"

"—You don't think I know that, Isa?" He leans forward, dropping his tone to a low whisper. "And that's not even the worst of it."

"Great." I pick at my donut. I need carbs and sugar.

"Your husband?" he questions, and I pause. "Is my first cousin." My chewing stops.

Dead.

My breathing even stops because what. The. Fuck.

My hand begins to shake as a deep buzzing sound pierces through my eardrums. "Not possible," I whisper, dropping the donut back onto the plate like it was infected. Though by this point, I'd take an infection. If a demon possessed my body right at this very moment, I'd submit. *Yo, I tried this life shit, homie, now take me home.*

"Actually, it is. My mom and his mom are sisters." He leans back in his chair. "You weren't the only person who ran away to New Orleans for a chilled life, Isa."

Chilled life? If his mom is anything like Bryant's mom then he's deluded. I wonder idly why I'd never met his mom.

"I'm confused. How can this happen? How does this happen?" I shake my head. "It doesn't make sense."

"Well, I'm trying to figure out why he married you."

"Huh," I laugh, taking a sip of my coffee. "Well, it doesn't have anything to do with you, Devon. That much I can tell you."

"Isa... I've known Bryant all my life. It's not something I'm proud of and I don't go broadcasting our connection—as you know—" he adds at the end, casting a gentle look at me. "But I've known him since we were born and he's *not* a good man."

"He's not that bad, Devon."

That's a lie. He's all things bad, and even though I know Devon has known him longer, I don't feel comfortable with him talking about Bryant that way.

Devon scoffs. "Really? And you know this... how?"

I don't. But over the past couple days, I've been getting to know Bryant a lot. Slowly but surely his ice wall has been melting toward me, I can just feel it. Whether that ice wall melts and drowns me, we will see, but I also don't know what he and my father have that needed him marrying me. At least I'm not disillusioned with the thoughts of him being in love with me. I can't get hurt this way because I have no expectations out of this marriage, I've known what was going on from the beginning.

"I just do."

Devon shakes his head. "I can't do this with you, Isa." He stands from his chair and looks down at me, tossing some bills onto the middle of the table. "Unless you can see Bryant for what he truly is, I can't do this with you. I'm sorry." Then he walks out and leaves me there alone, gathering my thoughts. I feel like that was it. No matter what, Devon and I will never be how we used to be. We will never be as close as we used to be. That bridge has been burned and there's no going back from it. Finishing my coffee, I get up from my chair and walk out of the restaurant. Brian is still parked in the same spot and when he sees me he gets out of the front seat and opens the back door.

I smile, not being able to say anything else. "Thanks, Brian."

14

BRYANT

"A re you going to tell her?"

Isaac asks, smirking at me from across my desk.

"No."

He laughs. "I'm not surprised, but I am surprised with why..."

"What do you mean?" I snap, feeling myself begin to get annoyed at where his impending questions are coming from.

"Well, you had no issues telling her anything before. I want to know why the sudden shift in telling her now?"

"Because," I start, leaning back in my chair. "Because there's no need to tell her anything. She's compliant, for some fucked reason. I don't have to manipulate her."

"Tragic she actually doesn't mind being married to you." My fingers twitch from under my desk and thoughts of watching the life seep out of Isaac's eyes make butterflies erupt in my belly. This, again, isn't a good sign.

"Well, who wouldn't?" I grin, brushing him off while putting a cigarette in my mouth and lighting it. I blow out a thick cloud of smoke and relish in how all my tense nerves relax along with murder plots and alibis to killing one of my best friends.

"Well, I don't know. I know one girl who didn't," Isaac whips back. "Speaking of, she will be at the charity event this weekend, and I take it, you're taking Isa with you..."

I shrug, taking another hit of the nicotine. "Yeah, and what of it. Hayley wasn't anything special, Isaac."

Hayley means jack fucking shit to me up against how I feel about Isa.

"Really?" He arches a brow.

"Really," I deadpan. "We were kids."

Isaac gets up off the chair and shrugs. "Well, then I'll bring the popcorn. I'll put one hundred on Isa though, she's feisty as fuck."

I grin. My girl is rather feisty. Hayley was my high school friend slash girlfriend. We grew up together and then went separate ways when she went to Harvard law and I went into business. We didn't see each other for years until she made partner at a major firm here in NYC. She's in the big leagues, the woman is fierce in a courtroom—and in bed. But I haven't cheated on Isa, and I won't. This marriage may be more like a business arrangement, but Momma taught me better than that and anyway, I was fussy when I was single. What's the point of going out to get laid by women who have to tick all my boxes when I have one at home that doesn't just tick all my boxes but fucking shatters them open too, and the fact that she fucks like a pro is obviously also a bonus.

I put out my smoke and get up from my chair, walking out of my office. "Dahlia!"

My assistant comes out of the lunch room carrying a coffee. "Yes? Your next appointment isn't until four p.m. with

Samsung and everything you need has been printed and is waiting for you on your desk," she yaps off effortlessly, and this is exactly why I have the best assistant in the country.

I nod. "Thank you. I'll be back at four."

Strolling into the penthouse, I toss my keys on the table and loosen my tie. "Isa!" I need to lose myself in her for a few hours.

When she doesn't answer back, I make my way upstairs, grabbing a bottled water out of the fridge on my way. I know she's home because Brian is home. He was my personal bodyguard, and probably one of the only men I trust, hence why he's watching Isa. I push open our bedroom door and see her little body curled in the fetal position on the bed, facing the window.

"Were you going to tell me?" Her voice barely breaks above a whisper.

I narrow my eyes on her back. "Tell you what?"

"About Devon," she answers, her tone dead, flat, and defeated. I don't like this tone much, I prefer Isa alive and on fire. The hungry agro little spitfire I'm used to. I walk further into the room and come around the bed, taking a seat on the single Lazy Boy that sits beside the large window. I lean back and look at her face but she quickly swipes away the tears that had fallen down her cheeks.

Fuck. She's crying.

"Yes," I answer truthfully because I did plan to tell her, only that little piece of shit beat me to it. I lean forward. "I was going to tell you, babe, but honestly, it meant nothing to me at all. His existence is not why I married you or even why you were on my radar."

"Did you both set this up?" she further asks, pushing herself up and then crawling up the bed to lean against the headboard.

"What?" I'm honest to God slightly confused at her question.

"Well, I've been thinking..." she laughs sarcastically, her voice shaky from her crying. "Did you and Devon set up him being best friends with me in attempt to wife me? Was my friendship with Devon all a lie? Because honestly how can he just walk away from me."

I let out a soft growl, one that I'm sure she couldn't hear and then get off my chair to take a seat beside her on the bed. "Baby, you insult my resources when you throw around accusations like that."

"Oh, answer the fucking question, Bryant."

I chuckle, reaching out for her. "No, baby, no. I had heard about you through Devon before we were married yes, but I had thoughts of 'wife-ing' you well before he got his claws stuck into you." I end that sentence with my teeth clenched. Knowing Devon has had his dick inside of what's mine makes me edgy.

She looks at me and I fucking hate when she does that. Like if I lie to her, she'll know. I'm a businessman. I lie on a daily basis to some of the most powerful men in the world, but I can't lie to her.

Again, fuck.

"Okay," she answers softly and it throws me off. It throws me off because is that her trusting me? I've not given her any reason to trust me, in fact, I've probably done the opposite, but yet, she says 'okay.'

"Okay?" I look at her skeptically. "That's it?"

She nods. "Bryant, for this to work, I have to trust you, therefore, I will always ask you once and whatever you answer me with, I will always believe you. But the day that you lie to me will be the day that all trust is broken and I will never trust you again."

I tilt my head. "So why don't you ask me truthfully about the deal your father and I have?"

She shrugs, sliding off the bed. "I guess I don't want to use that to manipulate it out of you. I want you to trust me too." She pauses and looks at me over her shoulder just before she hits the closet. "And for you to do that, you have to open up to me in your own time." Then she disappears into the closet and I'm left sitting there, gobsmacked. I don't know what's happening between her and I, and I don't know how we went from being enemies to almost friends, but it's uncharted territory. Territory I'm not actually familiar with because I trust no one.

I get off the bed and make my way out of the bedroom. Yep, she'll be waiting a fucking long time.

15

Beeping sounds reverberated around the empty walls as I hitched up the heavy bundle in my arms.

"Dadadada..." the bundle of soft brown hair and rosy cheeks yapped off and I grinned down at her.

"That's right. Dada. Say it again..." I muttered as I continued to walk us down the silent hallway. Bleach and disinfectant fueled the air, and it took a while for me to get used to this smell, but after weeks of visiting, I've become accustomed to it and so has Harper. My heart cracks in my chest again when we stop outside of a door. Harper reaches forward, her little fingers going over the name that sits on the door.

"Mamama..." she gargles, dribble coming down her tiny little lips.

"Yes, baby. Mama."

I pushed open the door that reads "Isa Royal" on the front.

PULLING out some steaks that I have in the fridge, I hit dial for Brian with the Bluetooth speaker hooked up to my phone.

"Boss..."

"When does Maria get back?" Maria is my maid. She's been gone for two weeks now to be with family and I'm already ready to have her flight moved to an earlier date. I don't cook. Ever.

"Three days, sir."

I look into the empty fridge. "I think I need to do grocery shopping."

The phone goes silent, then Brian clears his throat, all though I can't see through the phone, I know he's smiling. "Send me a list and I'll do it. Can't imagine you in a supermarket."

"True," I answer. "I'll send you a list." Then I hang up my phone and scroll through Spotify, hitting play on old school Red Hot Chilli Peppers.

"Wow..." Isa teases, leaning against the frame of the kitchen island.

"What?" I fold my arms in front of myself, looking at her up and down while taking in how relaxed she looks in grey sweats and a little white tank top with her long hair falling down the side of her face and over her shoulder.

She grins, tilting her head. "Are you going to cook tonight?"

"I don't cook."

"You don't?" she mocks, and I know she's being sarcastic. She steps into the kitchen, rounding the bar and pulling out one of the stools. "I mean... my love for food is real, so I know how to cook all sorts of delicious food."

I smirk, maybe I don't need to fly Maria back early after all. "I've sent Brian to do some grocery shopping."

"I can do it," she replies, twirling her chair around to

face me before placing her face in the palm of her hands. Trying to be all innocent and shit. "I'm skilled at grocery shopping activities."

"Bet you are..." I mutter, closing the fridge door. "But no, he'll do it. You can cook while I'm at my four o'clock meeting with Samsung." I go back to the cupboards, taking down a couple of glasses and pouring wine into both.

Walking back to her, I wrap my fingers around her chin and tilt her face up to mine. "Are you okay?"

She searches my eyes in shock and then her shoulders deflate. "Yes. I think I'll be fine."

I now have two reasons to beat Devon's face in.

Leaning down, I kiss her on the lips as the front door swings open and I don't have to look to see who it is. "I need that fucking key back," I growl against Isa's lips and she chuckles.

Stepping backward, I grab my keys off the counter and wink at Isa. "See you later, baby. And you," I point to my bratty sister, "are *not* staying for dinner so don't get comfortable."

16

ISA

Well if you're cooking I won't be!" Jessica yells at the closing door. "Asshole," she further adds, walking into the kitchen and picking up Bryant's untouched wine that he had just poured.

I can't help it, I laugh, mainly because I love the dynamic between Jessica and Bryant. She keeps him on his toes, and it's sort of cute. "How's your day been today? Fucked any more bodyguards?" I quirk an eyebrow at her and she almost chokes on her drink.

"You know," she laughs after swallowing. "I pray every single day and I thank God for bringing you into our lives."

"Glad to be here." We toast and then take another drink.

"So, in all honesty, who is cooking?" she asks. "Because I know Maria isn't here, and the cupboards are looking pretty dry."

"Me!" I place my glass back onto the countertop. "I'm not bad at cooking. I love food, and I love eating. Obviously," I look down at my curves.

Jessica's eyes run down my body. "Pardon? Mrs. Size Two."

"Size four," I correct. "And that's a very hard to maintain size four. These curves? Are not the good kind. They're the kind that jiggle."

Jessica sighs, looking out into the distance. "I would kill for jiggly curves. I hate being petite."

"Oh," I roll my eyes. "Must be so terrible to be able to eat what you want and not put on weight." I want to punch her.

She laughs but looks down to her drink with a sad look casting over her face. "Yeah, I guess that's what most people think. But I've always had eating issues. Mainly eating disorders. When I look in the mirror, I see a whale, but people tell me I'm small, and don't," she shakes her head, "don't say 'oh you're being ridiculous, you're tiny,' I don't tell you this for sympathy or for you to tell me how skinny I am. It's just, I've always had a very bad relationship with food, even though I love to eat! I wish I could eat and it not impact how I view myself."

"Jessica..." I whisper sadly because I can't quite wrap my head around what she has just said. I've heard about these disorders, obviously, but to know that someone so close to me is struggling with it sort of hits home. "Well!" I get up off my stool, tipping the rest of my wine down my throat. "Looks like we're having nachos for dinner."

Jessica's eyes beam. "Really!"

I nod. "Uh huh."

She squeals, running around to me and wrapping me in her arms. "Best sister ever!" Then she pulls back and points back to my chair. "So!" Oh no. I look at her. "I hear that he took you to the rents' house. How'd that go?"

I laugh, relaxing slightly because she still doesn't know

about Justin. "Ah, it wasn't as bad as I expected. Though in my defense, I didn't know where we were actually going until we arrived at the house."

"The street name didn't give it away?" she asks with a judgey eyebrow quirked.

"Street name?"

"Yeah." She takes a sip of her wine. "It's called Royal Lane. They named it after my great-great whatever he was. Anyway, the house is old as fuck, and also, very haunted. I don't sleep in the main house when I do stay. I stay in the pool house."

Ahhh, that glorious pool house. My cheeks heat and my core clenches with the memories swimming in my brain.

"I knew it," I mutter, my eyes glazing over. "I knew that house felt haunted."

"Oh yeah," she adds between taking sips of wine. "It's very haunted."

I shiver, although I'm pretty sure the reasons why she says it's haunted has a lot to do with the history of the house and the age. Not really because of the same reasons as me.

The front door opens, and Brian walks through carrying armfuls of grocery bags. I chuckle, getting to my feet and going to help him. "Thank you, Mrs. Royal."

"Can I be miss Royal?" Jessica winks at poor Brian and he stiffens. "Ma'am, you are miss Royal."

Jessica rolls her eyes and takes out some grapes from one of the paper bags. "You call my mom ma'am, Brian."

Brian looks between both of us, and I wave him off, sensing his discomfort. Jessica Royal, a royal pain in the ass. "Thank you, Brian, but I don't suppose you could take us back to the store? I've decided to make nachos for dinner tonight so I will need to gather all the ingredients."

Brian nods. "I don't mind going back."

"No," I shake my head, rinsing my glass under the water. "We can go."

AN HOUR LATER, no shit, a whole hour to pick up mince, garlic, onions, red wine—plus more wine for while I cook— a tin of tomatoes, salsa, lettuce, sour cream, avocado, and some taco shells, and we're finally back home in the kitchen, waiting for the pan to heat up. Jessica hasn't let a single moment of silence pass between us during the entire time, but I appreciate it. It's keeping my mind busy.

Looking up at the time, I see it's almost five p.m., so it's a good thing nachos don't take long to cook. I don't know much about Bryant's meeting with Samsung, but if suits is any indication as to meeting times, even though Harvey Specter can talk, I'd say I'd be expecting him home soon.

"So what do you think?" Jessica mutters off, as I toss all the chopped onions and garlic into the pot to sauté.

"About what?" Pouring a glass of wine with one hand as my other is stirring the pot, I'm well within my element. Life is good, now all I'm missing is some good music. Just as I think it, Jessica hits play on Halsey "Bad at Love" and the speakers that are spread around the whole condo begin to play the song softly.

"About Jimmy!"

I crank my head over my shoulder to see what she's talking about, coming face to face with Jimmy. AKA some guy's Instagram account that is staring right at me. Well, more like his abs are staring right at me.

I go back to my cooking, throwing in the mince. "Are you asking me if I think he's hot? Because that's all I can go on right now, considering I've never actually met him."

"You think he's hot?" she asks again, and I turn my head over my shoulder to take another look, just to make her feel better, I don't actually need another look. He's not my type —period. The steroid enhanced arms, douchebag haircut and, not to mention, he takes selfies. Fucking selfies. Nope. Not allowed. Computer says fuck no. But I turn around to take another look for her sake.

"Mmmmm..." I pretend to ponder over her question.

"Be very careful with your next wording, wife, unless you want your ass beat."

My mouth snaps closed. "Aw, honey, you're home." I over exaggerate my smile at him as I stir the pot. Quite literally as well.

"Oh come on, B. I just want to know her answer."

His arm wraps around my waist and he yanks my body into him closer until I feel his cock press against my back. He leans down and licks my shoulder before biting on my earlobe and whispering, "You so much as acknowledge that piece of shit, I'll kill him, and then my sister, and then fuck you so hard that you'd wish I'd killed you too. You know, just to prove a point." He lets my speechless ass go and pops a grape into his mouth with a cheeky wink of an eye. "Yeah, *honey*, I'm home." Then he walks out, ripping off his tie and tossing it across the room.

This man.

For the love of all things that are unholy.

"Ohh," Jessica laughs while shaking her head and pouring more wine. "Homegirl, he owns you."

"Why," I moan, tilting the flute to my lips, "why am I attending, yet another charity event."

Jessica giggles, and then wiggles her eyebrows at me suggestively. "Maybe because of your choice of husband."

"True." Damnit. I didn't want to come to this event, but Bryant being Bryant, he was adamant on us making more appearances as a couple. Who would have guessed, but it turns out the united front means a lot to Bryant. I guess that's not too hard to believe though when you look at his mother and father.

My eyes automatically search for Bryant in the sea of overly priced frocks and hair extensions. After our dinner a couple nights ago, with Jessica in attendance, we've again, grown closer. I feel like the more time we spend together the more I want to be around him.

My eyes land on him talking to a woman with platinum blonde hair that's whisked up in a fancy high bun, a long red dress wrapping around her curves and those curves are of course to die for, and then she turns to face me with a smirk on her red lips before she leans into Bryant and whispers something into his ear.

Sipping my wine, I go to stand when Jessica's hand grabs my arm. "She's just history."

I look at Jessica's eyes seeing the sincerity in them before looking back to Bryant and the red witch. I glance back to Jessica. "Okay." Then I take a seat. I can't be mad at him. It's not like I'm the Virgin Mary. My knee jiggles under the table and I grab the champagne that's sitting in the middle, pouring another glass.

"Actually," I add, drinking the entire contents at once. "I'm feeling kind of tired. Can you let Bryant know I'll see him at home?"

Jessica seems to search over my face, trying to read my expression. She exhales. "Fine. Do you want me to come with you?"

I shake my head, placing my hand on hers and giving it a slight squeeze. "No. It's okay." Then I turn to walk out of the lobby and out the front sliding doors. I have to learn to trust Bryant. I can't act like a jealous wife, it will only embarrass him and give her too much satisfaction to know that she irks me. So I take myself home. Before I accidentally punch someone. That someone being the Red Witch.

"You ready to leave, Isa?" Jerry comes up behind me.

I smile, exhaling a long trail of pent-up anxiousness. "Yes, please."

After a long scrub in the shower, I pull open the bath-room door to find Bryant sitting on the edge of my bed. "Hey." I carry on, walking into the room, fluffing my damp hair up. I'm going to regret the decision to sleep with it damp immensely tomorrow.

"Why'd you leave?" he asks me, but his voice is different. Tortured. Confused. The room is dark, and the only light that is coming through is from the city lights that are sneaking through the floor to ceiling windows. He removes his tie and then shrugs off his dress shirt.

"I was just a little tired," I whisper, feeling the temperature in the room kick up a notch. Shit. Is he mad at me? Or did something happen after I left.

"Come here."

I follow his orders. He doesn't look up at me from where he's sitting, so I wrap my fingers around his chin and tilt his head up to face me, and that's when I see it. The undiluted confusion in his eyes. "I thought you were mad at me over Hayley."

I swallow.

Shaking my head, I whisper, "No," while running the tip of my index finger over the shadow of his beard. "I trust you."

His arm wraps around my waist and then he pulls me down, rolling his heavy body on top of mine, tugging off his pants and sinking into me with a hiss escaping his lips.

This sex wasn't fast. It was slow, sensual, and every time he pushed into me it was with a deep thrust. He continued the same torturous pace, locking his lips with mine and never letting up. He rode my body, and I rode his back from under him, all while our kiss never broke. Sweat dripped off of his forehead and would fall onto my face, and it was then

I realized this was the first time someone had ever made love to me.

17

I've just walked into the apartment after my gym session when I hear my phone vibrating on the kitchen bench. I'm surprised I could swing a gym session after all the love-making Bryant gave me last night.

"That thing has been ringing all morning!" Jessica groans, walking in with her hair all over the place and another man's shirt on.

"You just wake up?" I ask her in disbelief. It's eleven a.m.

"Shhh." She reaches blindly for the pot of coffee. Jeez, I really hope that isn't another bodyguard's shirt.

"Hello?" I answer my phone with a laugh toward Jess.

"Isa..."

"Devon?" Shock evident in my tone.

"Devon?" Jessica cocks her head, blowing on her new hot coffee.

"I need to talk to you. Can you come down to the lobby?" I look to a confused Jessica and then exhale. "All right, I'll be down in a second." Hanging up my phone, I look to her. "Long story."

"Is this my cousin Devon?"

I pause for a beat and then nod. "Yeah. It's a long story, but we've been friends for a very, very long time."

She seems to think over what I'd said, but the morning is obviously kicking her ass and the caffeine seems to be taking too long to take effect. "Just be careful."

"Why do you say that?" I ask lightly, throwing on my jacket and zipping it up now that my body has cooled back down completely from my HIIT training.

Jessica pauses again and then shakes her head. "I won't say anything, but just be careful."

Ignoring Jessica's warning, I walk down to the main lobby and I see Devon's lean back facing away from me outside. He looks to be watching all the passing cars. Putting one foot in front of the other, I make my way toward him, pushing the doors open.

"Hey!"

He turns to face me, his eyes rimmed red, his beard a little longer, and his shoulders slack. "I'm sorry, Isa," he murmurs, pulling me in for a hug. He squeezes tightly—almost too tightly.

I pause before bringing my hand up to his back and patting him lightly. "It's okay."

He gestures toward the long limo that is waiting for him at the curb. "I guess I'm using the family money now," he laughs, but his eyes don't smile, and his tone is barely above sad. "Want to go for a ride?"

"Sure." I pat his hand and slide into the backseat of the limo. I feel terrible about the way things Devon and I ended and it has been eating away at me since.

He slips in behind me and drops down on the seat opposite. "I'm sorry, Isa."

"Devon." I roll my eyes. "You can stop saying sorry now."

He shakes his head and looks out the window. "No, Isa, I can't, because this is the part where they take you."

18

BRYANT

My phone ringing cuts through the boardroom. Twelve sets of eyes all snap toward me. They're obviously waiting for me to apologize, which is when I decide that they're all idiots and I need to fire them. Muppets, I don't apologize to anyone and I especially don't in my damn boardroom.

"Hmmmm?" I raise my eyebrows at them all and slide my phone unlocked, spinning around in my chair to block everyone out.

"Jessica, I swear to God—"

"—B, it's Isa."

I pause, all thoughts about whatever merger we were exploring goes flying out the window. "What about her?"

"It's just, I'm probably overreacting, but you know me, I like—"

"—Cut the bullshit, Jessica and spit it out."

"It's Isa. She went out to see Devon about an hour ago and hasn't come back since. I'm worried because, well because it's *Devon*."

"Did you tell her about Devon?"

"What?" Jessica screeches down the phone and the way my ears pierce makes me want to beat her.

"Lower the fucking tone, Jess."

"Sorry," she murmurs and then drops it down a level. "But no, of course not."

I hang up and stand from my chair. "I've got to leave," I announce to the courtroom, though it really has fuckall to do with any of them.

"Ah, Bryant..." someone calls out from their chair, just as Dahlia looks at me from the glass window where her reception desk sits.

"It's my wife..." is all I answer, then I walk out of the room, leaving some important people in stunned silence.

I pass Dahlia's desk. "Cancel the rest of today and tomorrow."

"Ah, okay," she confirms, standing from her chair as I walk toward the elevators. "Bryant?" she calls out, as I hit the down button.

"What?" I look back at her, swallowing past the nerves and whatever the fuck this news has bought up inside of me.

"Please let me know if there's anything you need me to do."

I nod. "Thanks." She knows better than to ask a hundred questions. Stepping into the elevator, I pull my phone back out and dial Brian.

"Sir, we're on it."

"Why was she left alone?" I watch as the numbers go down, and it's as though someone's life is in the final countdown. That someone being Devon.

"I'm—I'm sorry, sir. I wasn't aware that she was going to see Devon or anyone, and neither was Jerry. It happened while I was parking the car after her morning training and Jerry doesn't come to the gym with her in the mornings."

I pinch my nose with my fingers. I can't blame Brian because I know that if it really came down to it, he would take a bullet for Isa, and not only because she's my wife, but because I've seen the way he looks at her. With adoration. As he would look at his daughter, and Isa would be around the same age as his daughter before she died in a car wreck a couple of years ago. He's never been the same since.

"I'll be there soon," I reply, then hang up the phone. The elevator dings open onto the main lobby and I run out, heading straight to the underground parking lot before getting into my Ferrari.

PUSHING OPEN THE PENTHOUSE DOOR, I look around desperately. Somehow, on the way over here, in between dodging cars and speeding past police officers, I had talked myself into thinking she would be here when I got home. I'd gotten so used to seeing her annoyingly bright smile and sassy fucking mouth every time I have entered the apartment since we got married, so I feel like today would be no different and she would be here when I got home.

My smile drops as soon as I see not just Jessica, but my mom and dad and Brian all in the living room with Jerry and three secret service agents huddled in the corner. They stand from their seats and I loosen my tie, closing the door behind myself.

"She's not here..." I whisper, more to myself than to anyone else.

Jessica shakes her head. "I'm so sorry, B. I honestly didn't think anything of it and the way that they talked on the phone—it sounded like they were close."

I silence her with a flick of my wrist. "They are—well, were close. She thinks the world of Devon, but I don't know what Devon thinks of her."

Tossing my tie onto the breakfast bar, I walk deeper into the room. She's with Devon, and worst of all, she doesn't know who Devon really is.

"Bryant, dear, we need to talk..." my mom cuts in softly.

"What? What are you both doing here anyway?" I look to Jessica. "You call them?"

Jessica shakes her head. "No."

I look back to both my parents. My mom's eyebrows are pinched together in distress and my father's eyes have drifted out to the floor to ceiling windows. The flicker of my gas fireplace that sits under the television illuminates the room in soft waves, and I exhale, dropping down onto the large couch. "Spit it out."

My mom hands me her phone and I take it from her while keeping my eyes locked on hers. "I swear to God if he has hurt her..."

She closes her eyes and looks away from me as if she's disappointed. When I look down to my phone, I understand why. There, staring straight back to me, are two completely lifeless grey colored eyes. Eyes I'm so familiar with. Blond hair is matted down on an oval face and with blood seeping through the strands of his hair.

"Shit."

"Did she do it?"

"What?" I hand back her phone. "Why would you ask that?"

"Because," my mom flicks through her phone again and then hands it back. I take it, narrowing my eyes at her and then looking back down to the photo that's spread out on her phone. It's a photo of Isa crying holding the weapon and looking at Justin's body in horror.

Who the fuck took these fucking photos.

I throw the phone across the sofa and lean back in the sofa, running my index finger above my lip. I don't give a fuck about their questions right now, right now, my sole focus is on finding Isa. I lean forward, burying my head into the palms of my hands while running my fingertips through my hair. I exhale. There's no reason why Devon would hurt her unless I'm missing something. Why would he take her? He gives a fuck about her, even I know that. There's no mistaking the way he looks at her, talks about her. I can see the adoration in his every word. I don't think he'd hurt her—no.

But then again...

No, this has to do with me.

"Bryant!" Mom snaps at me in an attempt to gain my attention. I ignore her. I don't care for their inquisitions right now.

"Bryant." Jessica's soft voice breaks through my hard shell, and my head snaps toward her involuntarily. It's true, my little sister drives me crazy on the best days but there's no one walking this earth that I care about nearly as much as I care about her.

"What?"

She steps toward me, bringing the palms of her hands to my face, her deep green eyes searching mine desperately. "Did she do this?"

I look back at her. "Yes—"

They all gasp, Jessica's hands falling to the sides of her.

"But!" I all but roar, my temperament kicking up from not only their questions but now their sudden disdain of Isa. "There is more to the story than you even know, and as much as I'd love to get into it right now, my wife has been kidnapped, so if you'd excuse me..." I barge past Jessica and she steps backward, her hand still covering her mouth. Heading into the kitchen, I open the top cupboard, taking down a heavy bottle of whiskey and a glass. Twisting the cap off, I pour some into my glass and toss it back before placing it back on to the bench. Taking my phone out of my pocket, I slide through my contacts just as Brian walks in.

"Do you need to make some calls?"

I need to do a lot of things, and calling people Is not one of them.

19

ISA

Devon..."

I let out a confused whisper, just as we pull down a busy side street of NYC. "Please..." I plead with him, but I see it when he looks away from me. I see that there's something else to Devon. Something confused and dark. Whatever he has planned to do with me, there's no going back. Feeling betrayed is not for right now. My betrayal will have to wait. The car stops outside of a brick building and Devon finally looks at me. "I'm sorry, Isa. But you made this choice."

"What does that even mean, Devon?" I glare at him while reaching for his hand in a sad attempt to bring out the Devon I know. The Devon I remember, because I don't even recognize this person.

He looks right at me. "The minute you agreed to marry him, your life was over. As far as they know."

I pull back my hand as if I touched fire. "What does that mean?" The car door swings open and a man dressed in a suit and dark glasses reaches in with a grin on his face. "How are we, kids? Isa? Come with me now."

"Who the fuck are you?" I snap at the suited man.

"I'm your worst nightmare."

"I doubt that," I mutter, getting out of the car while yanking my arm out of his grip. "I've met my worst nightmare, and I call him my husband, who by the way, will be hunting you right now."

His face drops. All cockiness eradicated from his features. "Get inside you little slut." He looks over his shoulder quickly. I can almost smell his fear, or maybe that was the smell of his tail tucking between his legs. If that ever had a smell, it would be a stench to bathe in right now.

I follow him to the heavy steel door. It swings open with another man standing in front, waiting for us to enter. What these men don't understand is that I'm trained for this. Being the president's daughter, I have been trained on how to handle every and any situation, but mainly we're trained how to handle a hostage situation. I know I have to remain calm and collected. Follow instructions, but there was always one rule that I could never be trained in—and that's keeping my mouth shut.

We walk through the entryway and I pause, looking down the long dark hallway. He shoves me again from behind just as the door closes behind him.

"Keep walking until I say stop."

Rolling my eyes because I'm well aware he can't see me, I continue toward the end of the hallway, ignoring the chills that set off over my spine. I just have to survive. It smells like damp sewer in here which isn't a good sign. Bryant would have called my dad and he will be searching for me. Hell, the best of the best will be searching for me. Just... stay alive and see what these people want.

We reach another steel door as the man that was following behind me comes in front, it swings open.

"Hey, sexy." Brooke's face came into view. Looking me up and down, she twirled her hair between her fingers. "You miss me? I hope so because I want to play."

BRYANT

I have a team already looking for her." I tug at my hair in frustration, leaning back into my chair and blazing up a smoke. It's been hours now, and still nothing. Nada.

"Well, I'll send out some codes too," Isa's father says through the voice box of my speakerphone. I lean forward in my leather chair, looking around my office as memories of the night before assault my brain. I made fucking love to her.

Fuck! The memories are going to fuck me up more than her presence ever did. I have to get her back.

"You don't seem awfully stressed for a man who has just been told his daughter has been kidnapped."

"Kidnapped is a strong word to use."

My blood turns ice, my face to stone. "And what *exactly* does that mean?"

"It means that this is Isa. She has probably run off, but I will do my best to find her. Again."

Shaking my head, I laugh. "She hasn't run off. Devon

took her. When was the last time she ran off, huh? When she was a kid?"

Silence. "Summer 2012."

More silence. My smirk drops. That was the time I met her, it was that summer. The day itself isn't as clear as I'd like it, but I remember her. I remember her wanting to get into trouble. The concert we had all attended in the paddock behind the tent had long since died down, but we watched her the entire time. I knew who she was and who her father was, and initially, we wanted to fuck with her a little. See how the man who was running for president's daughter ticked. See what I needed to do to get her on my side when the time came. But that all turned to shit quite fast when she killed Justin.

"Huh," I mutter. "That was when I met her."

"I figured," her father murmurs. "Look. I'm not saying that we should be worried, but considering the circum-stances around the marriage too, I wouldn't be surprised if she has run off."

Leaning back in my chair, I crank my neck and close my eyes. "We were...good...."

"What?"

"We were... good. We were starting to get on and build a connection. I don't think it's that."

More silence. All I can hear is the ticking of the old grandfather clock that is in the corner of my office. Fucking hate that thing. Stupid old piece of shit.

"I'll send out some feelers. You keep doing your bit." Hanging up the phone, I loosen my tie and toss it across the room.

Where the fuck is she.

21

ISA

Beep

.

Beep.

Cold chills lash out over my flesh, and I inch over, ready to throw up as a deep throbbing begins inside my brain.

"Brooke!" A scream shredded out of me as I pressed myself up from the concrete floor.

"Ohhh, come on, Isa," her seductive voice slithered from somewhere in the distance. "You know how much I like to play."

"Stop." I shook my head. "I don't want to play." I bang on my head, scrunching eyes closed. "I don't want to play, I don't want to play. Playing is for losers."

There was a long pause, so I lifted my head slowly, attempting to clear my eyesight. I saw her fuzzy form drop to her knees beside me. "But I want to." She leaned down, her lips touching mine softly. I squeezed my eyes shut and refuse to open them.

"No, Brooke. Don't touch me."

Her fingers wrapped around the back of my neck as she pulled my face into hers harder, until my lips cushioned against hers. Her tongue slipped inside my mouth but I bit down on it until the metallic sting of blood slipped down my throat.

She laughed, a psychotic giggle erupting from her chest. "Yes." She slipped back, swiping the blood off her bottom lip and then pressed the tip of her finger to my mouth. "Taste it, Isa. Taste what you've done. You know how I like it." Then she cranked her head, as I tried to keep my food down. She leaned in until her lips are brushing over my ear. "Do you love the taste of my blood?"

I knew what I needed to do in order for Brooke to leave me alone, but I wouldn't be doing it today—or ever.

"No, Brooke. We've only ever done this when another guy was involved and when we were drugged up."

She bent her head, a dark look flashing over her eyes. "Good thing I came organized then." Something stabs into my thigh and I scream, clutching it tightly.

"Isa..." a voice breaks through my hazy confusion, but I can't see anything. All my vision is met with is a murky mix of colors and a voice I don't recognize.

"You see," Brooke stood from the ground, "you weren't supposed to marry anyone, Isa." Her face came near mine but doubled. Her body actually fucking doubled, or maybe I saw triples.

I tilted my head slightly, and that's when numbness took over. "What did you stab me with!" I yelled, or did I? I wasn't sure. It felt like a yell, but then again I didn't hear anything. Then just as I realized I've lost my hearing, a loud buzzing zips through my eardrums.

"Fuck!"

"Isa! Don't let go!" another woman's voice comes in, and who the fuck is that! Why can't I see. Oh, this is a bad trip. What did Brooke drug me with.

Tossing and turning my head while fighting the blackness that's seeped in and out, I tried to fight myself into staying awake.

I have to stay awake, I must. Turning to face the door, I watched as a dark shadow entered, closing it behind himself. "You were supposed to be ours, Isa. We were supposed to have a baby together. You, me, and Brooke."

Devon. What the fuck was he talking about? My stomach flipped upside down and my throat clenched. I must be dying.

"No..." I fought it, just as darkness sucked me in and everything went black.

Dark fog.

"Isa! Please. For me. Please!" That same woman. That same voice.

Pain.

My eyes opened slightly, catching Devon right there on top of me, sweat dripping off his face with his eyes wide on mine as he thrust inside of me. Deep. He kept thrusting deep and hard. "I." Thrust. "Told." Thrust. "You." Double thrust. "Mine." Slammed into me and tears prickled out the side of my eyes. His cock pulsed inside of me and I had to fight the bile that was rising in my throat, although I didn't want to fight it. I wanted to spew all over his ugly fucking mug. How did I not know the Devon had this side to him? He hid it so well.

"My turn," Brooke grinned, ripping Devon's naked flesh off of my equally naked flesh.

"No!" I screamed, consciousness slowly seeped in. I could feel my muscles twitch as they awakened, but I didn't want to let her know. If I made it too obvious that the drugs had worn off, she might've given me more. I'd need to play drugged still. That'd be the only way.

Devon stood to his feet, yanking up his jeans. "We will keep her here until I know that she's pregnant."

"Isa, baby, please, please. Shit. Shit!" That voice again, but before I can register, my mind goes into a downward spiral of warped flesh and bright colors.

Brooke ran the palm of her hand up my inner thigh, swiped at Devon's leftover cum that had trickled out of me and slipped down my leg, and brought her finger to her mouth, sucking it clean off. There was no fighting it this time, I lurched over and gagged all the contents out of my belly.

"Gross," Brooke muttered, but her hand went back to my inner thigh as she pressed the nub of her thumb against my clit. Ugly wet tears fell down my cheeks now. I wanted Bryant. I missed him and I needed him. I needed his arms wrapped around me and I needed his fucking stupid grin smiling at me from across the room. Brooke straddled my lap. I internally talked myself down because my anger had hit new highs. Rage. Pure rage was pounding through my body.

She started to grind herself on me and that's when I took my chance. Launching my fist back, I pound it into her mouth.

"Yes! That's it, Isa! You've got this. Fight it, girl!" I need to know who this woman is. But the spiral is back.

"Agh!" she screamed, flying off of me and falling back on her ass while swiping the saliva and blood from her lips. "You fucking bitch!" She charged toward me, her fist reared backward before punching me in the face. A crunch whipped around the silent cold room and my head snapped back from the impact. Warm liquid gushed from my nose, seeping down the front of my chin and over my naked chest.

"Brooke!" I wanted to fucking kill her. I wanted to watch as the life got sucked out of her eyes.

"Shut up!" she screamed, lifting her leg and booting me square in the face. My head snapped back and I fall backward. Throbbing numb pain starts to vibrate over the back of my head as everything started slipping in and out of consciousness again.

No. Fuck off. I am not going down like a little bitch.

"Tsk tsk, Isa..." she laughed, tilting her head back.

Beep.

Beep.

That fucking sound again.

"You thought you could escape me?" Brooke laughed as I *struggled to keep my eyes open, the assault of a bright light booming in front of my eyes. I threw my arm up to shield from the assault. I reached for the crowbar that was beside me and got to my feet. Rearing it backward, I stabbed the sharp end of it through her chest.*

"Fuck you!" I roared, with so much release of hate, I dropped to the floor. She clutched her chest and fell to her back. The sounds of her choking on her own blood like a sweet lullaby to my frantic thoughts.

"Isa!" I know that voice.

"Bryant?" I squint my eyes toward the light, but before I can make out the shape of whoever it is that's there, Bryant comes running inside. "Don't move!"

My eyelashes are flicking, everything coming back into view clearly.

"Bryant grips my arm while wrapping his suit jacket around my bare chest. "Get up, baby. Can you move?" I look around then back to Bryant and nod, standing tall on my feet. I swipe the tears off my face, eying a long crowbar that has just been tossed to the side in the corner of the room. *I went straight toward it, picking up the rusted handle and swinging it over my shoulder before turning back toward Brooke.*

She laughed, her head tilting back. "Oh what? You really think you can hit me with that thing? I can't die, Isa." Launching my elbow back, I grinned. "Yep." Before slamming it across her head. She dropped to the ground as blood begins to ooze out of her head.

"Isa..." Bryant whispers into my hair, but I can't respond because all of a sudden

Blackness seeps in and I drop to the ground.

22

W hat do you mean?"

Bryant? Is that him talking?

"I mean, it's complicated..." That's my dad —no doubt.

"How so? Explain. I have time."

"It's just, Isa is troubled."

"I know she's troubled!" Bryant's voice kicks up a notch, and I flinch inwardly. "That's what the fuck I find so sexy about her."

"Okay, there's a few things wrong with that statement." Is that my sister? What the hell is she doing here. "What my father is trying to say, is that she's a little more wild than the average girl. But I'm sure you already know that."

Long pause, and then the mattress sinks under some- one's weight.

"Of course I know that," Bryant mutters, before softly adding, "But she's mine."

My heart soars inside my chest at those words coming out of Bryant's mouth. I'm his. Not too long ago, I was driving him crazy, now he's jumping up and claiming me on the first go. Slowly, I feel my skin tingle and their talking becomes louder.

My eyes open. "Hey." Pressing myself off the hospital bed, I rub the sleep from my eyes.

"Oh thank fuck!" Bryan turns to face me, his hand coming to my face. "How you feeling?"

"Good...I think." I look around the room to find not just Bryant and my parents there, but Bryant's parents and sister too.

His mom comes to my bed, taking my hand in hers. "We don't blame you, Isa." Through my tears, I look around the room until I see Jessica, who is now coming toward me.

"Sisters are better than brothers anyway."

"Hey!" Bryant scolds her.

I laugh, swiping the tears off of my cheeks and casting a small look to my sister who was curled up in a ball on the other side of the room, tears pouring down her face. "Yeah, they totally are."

"Please take me home."

"Renewing your vows? Like, who even does that?" Brianna scolds, straightening my hair from the back.

"Us, of course. And you already know how we don't do

anything by the book, Bri." She pauses, putting the brush back onto the dresser.

"You're right." She brushes off a piece of my hair from my shoulder. "I'm sorry. I think pregnancy is making me cranky."

"Hey!" I laugh. "I've been pregnant too, and you didn't see me breathing fire." She steps back and laughs. "You were a freak of nature. When I hit that third trimester, damn. You get fat, swollen, cranky, and don't even get me started about the confusion of your sex drive. Do you want it? Or not? You need it but the thought of it grosses you out and then there's the fat thing again, and the hungry thing so you jus—"

I zone out of my sister's stupid ramblings and look back at myself in the mirror. After the Brooke and Devon ordeal, it's been a rough year, but through it all, Bryant and I have never been stronger. It was his idea to renew our vows since I gave birth to Harper last week. I know, everyone had asked me if I was crazy getting remarried in my post-pregnancy state, but none of that matters to Bryant and me.

Collecting up the rest of my belongings, I head for the door with Briana behind me. "You look casual," she says calmly, looking at my body up and down. "But you look mighty fine for just having a baby!" She's right, I do look casual, but I don't look fine. That's her pregnancy eyes kicking in. I'm walking down this time in nothing but a loose nude dress that hangs around my knees. I never wanted the damn big dress anyway.

"Yes, that's the plan. I didn't want extravagant, I just wanted. Me. I wanted Bryant. I wanted us."

Brianna looks me straight in the eye and smiles a sad smile. "Let's do this."

· · ·

SLOWLY WALKING down the dimly lit aisle, I clutch the bouquet of lilies in my hand. It's around eight p.m., so the sun has long since set and all that we have as lighting are the candles beaming up the aisle and all the fairly lights that are dangling above the seating area in the large trees, before finally trailing up around the altar. I look up to see Bryant cradling baby Harper in his arms and eying me in such a way it has my skin prickle, my heartbeat race, and sweat to bead out of the pores in my skin. Bryant is an incredible father. He puts new meaning to "Daddy." Seeing him play with Harper has my lady bits tingling where they definitely should not be tingling one week after giving birth. Even if I did need a C-section.

Shit. I let out a long exhale of pent-up air just as my feet reach the altar.

This is it. This is my life, my beautiful, insane, very fucked up life. But it's mine and I'm the luckiest girl in the world.

"Mr. and Mrs. Royal, we're gathered here today...."

Beep.

Beep.

Author note: If you're satisfied with the image this story has given you, please stop here, as you're about to get a rude awakening.

23

B *eep*
.
  Beep.
Beep.

What's that sound? I look around, out to all our guests who are seated in their seats. What is that sound? My eyebrows tug in in confusion and I look back at Bryant.

"What's wrong?" he asks, his face blurring like a fuzzy TV show that's struggling to gather enough signal. A woman, standing in the shadows behind the tree comes into view, and I put my hand over my eyes to try to shade my view onto her. "Hey!" But she runs away.

"I—I—" I look out to our guests again, only they begin melting away. "What?" I whisper, my hand coming up to my forehead.

Beep.
Beep.
Beep.
The trees all melted together in a puddle of wet goo, and

when I looked back to ask Bryant what was going on, he was gone.

But there was someone there. Brooke stared back at me with a smirk, dangling a machete in front of her.

"Well, well, well..." She swung her arm back and launched the sharp side of the machete deep into my throat. Blood seeped down the side of my throat and I dropped to the floor, clutching my neck. Choking on the warm liquid that was filling my mouth, Brooke stepped over me as my vision came in and out.

This was bad.

I was going to die.

Where was Bryant? Oh my god, Harper! And who was that woman? Tears poured down my cheeks.

"Where—where—" I muttered, but failed because the blood was coming in so much faster now. So much faster.

"Bry—"

Brooke laughed, then launched her arm back. She grinned. "I win."

Everything went black.

"She's not coming back."

Beep.

"Good riddance."

A blood-curdling scream tears out of my mouth as I launch off the hospital bed.

"Nope, she's back," someone says beside me and exhales, taking a seat on one of the chairs.

"Where am I?" I look around the sterile white room, my eyes narrowing.

"Isa..." the weird man dressed in a white gown growls beside me. It's then that I realize I can't move my hands because they're wrapped around my waist by a straitjacket. "Isa, it's ok... we've done this so many times—remember? I'm Mr. Barrack, and this is nurse Turner. You're still in the institution here at Merry Hill."

"What?" I snap, shocked. Confused. Institution? What the fuck.

"Isa."

"Stop calling me Isa!" I roar at them all, and that's when I catch my reflection in the bleak window. "Oh my God! No...." I shake my head.

The doctor pauses and reaches for a panic button. "Justine..." he whispers to the nurse discreetly, his face pale while reaching for the panic button. "Justine, get help." Then he looks back to me. "Brooke? Is that you?"

"Of course it's me!" I yell. "Why the fuck am I in this fugly slut's body!"

The doctor turns pale and in one quick rush, he slams the palm of his hand on the panic button before whispering, "I never...she lost..." His shoulders dropping. "Isa lost."

"Yes," I smirk, finally realizing what he means. "And I won." With all the power I can muster, I rip off the straight jacket, reach for the vase beside my bed and smash it against his head. "I wooooonnnnnnnn!" I roar, just as a dozen officer's rush into the room and launch me back into my bed, injecting me with serum.

.   .   .

"JUSTINE," Mr. Barrack whispers, taking a seat beside the shaken nurse in the main lobby. "It's going to be ok."

"Isa's really gone?" Justine mutters, swiping her eyes. "No more telling her stories."

"She's gone. But she'll be at peace now. She's resting with the wild stories that live in her head. Remember she suffered daily, Justine. What we've done, we've only done to help her get through those days. I mean reliving the same story inside your head every single day? That's a lot to take on for a schizophrenic."

"We never were sure if she was a schizophrenic, though," Justine adds. "It could be psychosis."

"But she lost, that's what we know. The good person lost in this story. You know, in the four months that she was dropped here out of the blue, I felt a connection to her."

"She did lose, and I too, felt a connection to Isa, but Brooke must have killed her. There's no other explanation. I hated Brooke's visits. She's vile."

Justine smiles, swiping her eyes. "Isa was a great girl. Told a good story. I swear, her story will never get old. Bryant and Isa. We can only dream to have a relationship like that, and Isa did. Daily." Justine fought back all of her emotions that were surrounding her.

"She was special." Mr. Barrack adds sadly. "But unfortunately, we can't win them all. Sometimes," he looks over his shoulder and toward the door which leads you into where Isa's padded room was.

"Sometimes the bad people win."

24

BRYANT

Shhh,"
I coo into Harper's soft brown curls as I toss my hoodie over my head. "You need to be quiet, baby." For being just over four-months old, she sure spoke a lot. I pause as I reach the door and look into the little window. I see her, Isa, sitting on the bed with her legs crossed and her head tilted. The straight jacket is wrapped tightly around her and just as I go to turn the door handle to let myself in, the way I've always snuck myself in, which always included Jerry and some secret service agents, Isa's lip curls up in a sadistic smile that sets chills out over my spine.

That's not Isa.

That's Brooke.

My heart sinks and a ball of sadness rolls in the pit of my throat.

I lost her. After all this time, after all the fight I put in, I lost her.

I tuck Harper into my hood and run out the long corridor of the institution.

It's just us now.

Just us.

My phone vibrates in my pocket, and the name "The Reaper" displays across the screen. I slide it to unlock. "Devon. We need to fucking talk."

The End

(for now)

ABOUT THE AUTHOR

amojonesbooks.com
amojonesauthor@yahoo.com

Printed in Great Britain
by Amazon